THE SPIDER:
SLAVES OF THE DRAGON

THE MASTER OF MEN!

SPIDER®

SLAVES OF
THE DRAGON

By Grant Stockbridge

STEEGER BOOKS • 2020

CHAPTER 1
SEAL OF DOOM

WENTWORTH STOOD well back from the crowd and airily swung his sword-cane, back and forth. His pose was casual. It was his habit to go into battle with his body and his brain at ease. And battle might well be at hand! To Wentworth's keen mind, it seemed more than a little strange that a police raid on a lingerie shop should be guarded by a machine gunner whose twitching, white face betrayed a dope addict!

For that matter, it was strange that this lingerie shop—one of the city's most exclusive, and located in the most fashionable part of Madison Avenue—should be raided at all... Yet there could be no mistaking the nature of the police errand. A procession of women was being hustled to the patrol wagon at the curb by a file of men in blue. Above the jeering of the growing crowd, Wentworth could hear the wailing and weeping of the prisoners. As he watched, one women wheeled toward a guard and raked at him with clawed fingernails. There was a downward blur of the man's arm and a nightstick smashed her to the pavement.

Wentworth's breath caught in his throat. He settled his hat firmly on his head, gripped his cane lightly in both hands and started a swift circuit of the crowd. It was not his custom to interfere with police business, but abruptly he did not believe these men were police! Quite aside from the thing he had witnessed,

Policemen, firemen and internes were
carrying the helpless victims!

from the appearance of the machine gunner, crouching tensely now over his weapon on the back step of the patrol wagon, Wentworth had ample reasons for suspicion. Within the last

week, there had been three mass kidnappings on the streets of New York, groups of young girls snatched into waiting cars and carried off before those who had witnessed the attack could even shout an alarm! There had been no demands for ransom; in most cases there were no wealthy relatives to pay. The entire chain of vicious crimes was shrouded in deep mystery… It seemed fairly obvious that this was another of the same bold kidnappings!

The temper of the crowd had entirely changed since that brutal clubbing. They had jeered at the women; now they booed and hissed the cops, and there was sullen anger in their tones. Men opposed Wentworth's advance until they met his steady eyes, saw the firm set of his lips; then they gave way. He burst through at a spot directly beside the machine gunner and the man whirled, punched the muzzle of the tommy-gun against Wentworth's chest!

"Naw you don't!" be grated raspingly. "Just get back there with the rest!" His lips shrank back from his teeth.

Wentworth smiled, masking the anger in his eyes. "I am Richard Wentworth," he announced pleasantly. "I have a card from Commissioner Kirkpatrick. You must know, of course, that I have special privileges."

There was a nervous tic at the corner of the machine gunner's mouth which twitched the whole side of his face. He was hopped up to the ears, crazy with the cocaine or heroin he had snuffed, mad with the fever to kill. The jerk of a man's hand might cause him to shoot. And a jerk of the hop-head's finger would saw Wentworth in half with bullets!

"I don't know you," the gunner snarled. "You get back there with the rest."

WENTWORTH STILL smiled, watching the women herded one after another into the waiting prison van. Several of them were obviously models for the shop. They wore only the briefest of underclothing beneath the coats they had thrown on. Patently, the models offered the excuse for this false raid.

"Where's your sergeant?" Wentworth asked the man. "He'll know about me."

The man hesitated. "All right," he agreed finally. "The sergeant's up there at the door."

Wentworth pushed along between the ranks of the mob. He did not turn his head, but he knew that the muzzle of that sub-machine gun was aimed between his shoulder blades, following him as he walked! A touch on the trigger, and…!

A man with sergeant's chevrons stood against the wide show window of the shop. He had a broad grin on his face as he made his men hurry the women along. Wentworth chanced a hidden glance at the machine gunner, saw that the weapon was still trained hungrily on his back! Well, he'd have to risk that….

"Get along with yez!" the sergeant cried cheerfully. "Sure, I know you're only a customer, lady, but we'll need you to give evidence. Nope, can't just give your name and go home on account of how would I know it was the right name? What are you crying about, baby? Of course, I can't give you time to dress. The way you ain't dressed is evidence… What the hell do you care who sees you like that? Ain't you been exhibiting yourself to anybody what comes into the shop, and without the coat, too?"

Wentworth frowned. The attitude of the machine gunner was suspicious, but the sergeant sounded authentic. Wentworth's eyes went beyond him to the policeman who stood against the shop window nearby. That officer had been deprived of his nightstick, which the sergeant waved jauntily, and there was a blackening swelling about his left eye. He was darkly sullen....

The sergeant turned to the crowd. "What's the hell's the matter with yez? Keep quiet before I make you move on. Sure, I know the copper hit the lady, but I hit him back, see?" He gestured toward the sullen man's puffy eye. "Besides, he'll get his before the trial board...."

He spotted Wentworth, took a short step toward him. "What do you want? Get back there with the rest!"

Wentworth opened his wallet and showed the police card his friend, Stanley Kirkpatrick, Commissioner of Police, had given him. The sergeant touched his cap's visor respectfully.

"What can I do for you, Mr. Wentworth?" he inquired pleasantly.

Wentworth jerked his head toward the machine gunner and saw that he was tautly ready to shoot, his face tight. Wentworth's own face didn't show his certainty that the man was eager to kill him, he would fire....

"Did you know, Sergeant," he asked, quiet-voiced, "that your machine gunner is hopped to the ears?"

He watched the sergeant, and the man's astonishment seemed genuine. His mouth fell open. *"Doped?"* he gasped. "The divil you say! I'll disarm him!"

The last of the women was being thrust into the patrol wagon, now, and the men in uniform were getting into other cars in which they had descended on the shop. The sullen cop with the injured face slouched along with them.

Wentworth smiled at the sergeant. The man certainly was

disarming. He doubted that any crook could put on such a clever act. "Better be careful, Sergeant. You know how these snowbirds are. Perhaps you'd better..." Wentworth's eyes were gazing absently at the numbers above the sergeant's golden

shield. Suddenly they came into clear focus... *What the devil?*

A coldness crept into Wentworth's blood. He knew that shield number, and it did not belong to this man! It belonged to Wentworth's friend, Tim Mulvaney...!

Wentworth could not be mistaken about the number, and there could be only one interpretation. This man, who wore Mulvaney's shield, or its duplicate, was an impostor! The whole thing was a fake and these were kidnapers! Although Wentworth's face was expressionless, the false sergeant must have guessed that something was wrong from his abrupt quietness. Wentworth saw the impostor's hand slide toward his gun, but he was wearing unaccustomed clothing. Even if he had held the weapon in his hand, he would have had no chance. Wentworth did not wait to draw. His left hand lanced out, caught the man's tunic just below the collar. He whirled him about between himself and the machine gun and clicked the head of his cane, jutting from his right fist, to the man's jaw!

THE FALSE sergeant's head snapped back on his shoulders; his body went loose, but did not collapse. Wentworth dropped his cane and his hand flew to the gun beneath his left arm. An

7

instant before the man sagged against him, his automatic leaped clear of its holster. It had all happened in a heartbeat of time. Even the men in the front rank of the crowd did not understand what had occurred. The man with the machine gun didn't have to understand. He saw quick movement and his finger tightened convulsively on the trigger of his weapon. The first stuttering slugs hammered into the back of the false sergeant, each one striking with a force of more than a quarter-ton in foot pounds. It hurled him headlong against Wentworth and the continued blows drove him to the ground with the fake sergeant on top of him. Pain jarred the impostor out of his daze and he screamed, piteously and horribly, into Wentworth's face while his arms and legs threshed. Wentworth fought to get his gun clear, to burn down that wild murderer with the machine gun. There were other screams now, the shrieks of panic-stricken men and women, dying under the lash of burning lead. The cackling death-laughter of the tommy-gun seemed to fill the world!

With a bitter curse, Wentworth brought his automatic hard against the head of the dying sergeant whose body shielded him from death. The threshing became a quiver and Wentworth could get his head clear and lift his gun. His accuracy was an instinctive thing. He had trained his hands until they scarcely knew how to miss, even if he wanted them to. He willed his gun to kill now and his slug caught the machine gunner between the eyes, hurled him backward to the street. The tommy-gun arched through the air, crashed into the crowd.

As if Wentworth's shot were the starting gun of a race, the automobiles of the kidnapers lurched forward. The siren of the

The slug caught the machine gunner between the eyes!

patrol wagon tocsined into the noon-day traffic, split a lane for escape. Wentworth rolled his human shield away, staggered to his feet. He brought up his gun deliberately and fired once at the last of the fleeing cars. The blasting hiss of an exploding tire echoed his shot and the sedan swerved like a shying horse, climbed a lamp post, teetered, crashed over on its side. For a moment, save for the retreating wail of the patrol and the shrill screams of the wounded, there was no sound in all the street. Then there was a strangled shriek, and one of the uppermost doors of the wrecked car banged open. A man exploded from the opening, danced about on the pavement, gripping his throat with both hands. They could not stop the crimson flood. He pitched forward on his hands and knees, then sagged to the pavement. His screams stopped. No other man left that wreck.

Wentworth had been casual when he began the battle, but there was nothing careless about his pose now. There was white fury on his face. He flung a swift glance about him. The bodies of men and women were strewn bloodily upon the pavement with that peculiar inertness which marks those who are violently dead. A woman screamed, a single hoarse note, as she tried to drag herself along on stiffened forearms. Her legs trailed helplessly. A man lay flat on his back, glaring up at the glaring sky. His face was twisted with suffering, but he uttered no sound. A curse born somewhere within Wentworth's vitals exploded from his lips.

HIS HAND whipped to his vest pocket. He stooped beside the dead sergeant and pressed the base of a platinum cigarette lighter to the man's forehead, then straightened stiffly, settling his hat upon his head, shrugging his coat shoulders smooth. He had his cane again and his gun was back in its holster. There was a bitter thinness about his firmly chiseled lips. It was a foolhardy thing he had done, with his cigarette lighter—but it could not be undone now. In his own person, in a spot where he might readily be recognized, he had imprinted on a man he had slain—*the seal of the Spider!* If he were identified with it… *Richard Wentworth would surely die!*

It was as simple as that. Richard Wentworth was a wealthy clubman, a superb sportsman, dilettante of the arts, an amateur criminologist… The Spider was a hunched and sinister figure who moved across the ominous background of the Underworld, an avenger who brought swift death to those who preyed upon humanity. The Underworld hated him, hourly sought his death. The police would drag him before the tribunals of their justice for a hundred killings. Yet those two, Wentworth and the Spider, were one man. He was lost if anyone could prove he had seen him print his spider-shaped crimson seal upon the brow of this man who so richly deserved to die. It was his warning to the vicious criminals who were kidnaping women. The Spider was on their trail!

Wentworth flung a glance about him, reached the curb with quick strides. The street was deserted, swept clean by that slaughtering gun. Those who had not fallen before its bullets had fled, but already they were creeping back. If they found the Spider here beside a dead man who bore his seal… There was nothing more he could accomplish here. The fleeing kidnapers' siren was dimming with distance and soon ambulances would be here to

11

care for the wounded who still survived. The Spider's duty sped him on the heels of the fugitives. A taxi… He stooped and pulled a police whistle from the sergeant's breast pocket, moved with long, lithe strides along the street. Surely, at the corner… The swift tattoo of a woman's heels pursued him, a woman running. He did not slacken his pace, nor did he look back. If she had not already seen his face… The heel taps drew swiftly nearer!

"Oh, please!" a woman's voice called. "Please, wait…!" Her voice was husky, but rich and cultured of tone. "Please, wait…" A hand clutched at his arm. "You are going after them! Take me with you!"

Wentworth's lips tightened with impatience, with a hint of desperation, too. He had violated his long declared rule never to use the Spider's seal while in his own identity, and this was the result. He had been spotted, and it might well mean his death! If this woman had seen him use the seal, if she told her story to authorities… Her footsteps kept pace with him, running to match his strong stride.

"Please, you must take me with you! Those kidnapers took Lucy! Oh, my baby sister!"

Wentworth turned sharply, his gray-blue eyes burning. "Madam," he said, "I'll have to request you to let go of my arm. I'm not pursuing those men. I have other business to attend to."

The woman's eyes were dark, tragic. There was a quiver in her rich lips.

"You're lying!" she whispered. "You are going after them. Any true man would have to. And you…."

"No," Wentworth cried. "For God's sake, leave me…!" His

teeth set solidly together. His tension, the need for haste had betrayed itself in his cry... Wentworth realized abruptly that this was the woman who had been knocked down by the fake policeman's club. Her dark-brown hair streamed about her shoulders and where it caught the light, it showed glints of auburn. There was an angry bruise across her temple... Her lips tightened.

"You shall go after them!" she cried, her voice abruptly harsh, "and you'll take me with you!"

Wentworth stood still, staring into her face.

"You'll take me," she went on decidedly, "because I saw... what you did back there! I saw you use... *the Spider's seal!*"

CHAPTER 2
DOUBLE IN DEATH

WENTWORTH SMILED slightly at the woman's gasping accusation. She dashed on rapidly as if even the words frightened her, and with her straight, aristocratic nose, the firm set of her round chin, she was not a woman given easily to fear.... But there was no time for argument. The siren was almost inaudible. Wentworth caught the woman's arm.

"You are right and you are wrong," he said swiftly. "Come!"

A half-dozen strides took him to the cross-street and a taxi driver flinched back from a corner around which he had been peering. His cab was parked at the curb and Wentworth gestured him toward it, thrust the woman in and sprang after her.

"Straight up Madison," he ordered, "and keep your car wide open. Police business!"

The driver leaped to the seat, spun the taxi away from the curb and into Madison in one, long, sweeping movement. Wentworth leaned far out of the window and used the police whistle he had snatched from the false sergeant's pocket. He blew on it shrilly and continuously and the traffic divided for him. Traffic policemen leaped to clear a path for his cab. The sound of the sirens was drowned in the deep throb of the motor, but Wentworth knew the acoustics of his New York, was sure that he would not have been able to hear the siren so long if it had not kept straight along Madison Avenue. When they had gone a half dozen blocks, he began shouting at the traffic officers they passed.

"The patrol?" he cried, pointing to the side streets.

When they had gone eleven blocks, the traffic officer nodded violently to Wentworth's query and pointed down the side-street. It was too late for the taxi driver to turn that corner, but he whirled eastward at the next intersection and raced the wrong direction along a one-way street. The skirling police whistle sent cursing drivers to the curb and at Park Avenue the taxi cut southward, split the two-lane traffic wide open and spurted eastward across town once more.

The driver twisted his head about, "Always wanted a chance like this!" he yelled. "Boy! Am I good!"

"Look out, fool!" Wentworth barked and the driver just dodged a truck barging out of a loading pavilion. The hunch of his shoulders grew tense and he kept his eyes rigidly forward. Wentworth smiled slightly. All men could become power drunk. The driver was feeling that intoxication now…. The smile twisted. And the criminals behind these kidnappings were mad on the brew of easy money! God help the Spider to strike swiftly and well today for the sake of the humanity he long ago had pledged himself to serve.

The sound of the siren, spurting occasionally, came to Wentworth even above the motor. They had gained on the patrol wagon. He stopped whistling and dropped back on the seat. His lips felt dry.

"When you sight that patrol wagon, go right on past," he told the driver, "then turn a corner and stop. They're not police, but crooks in police uniforms."

The taxi driver nodded stiffly, but did not again twist his head about. Wentworth turned quietly toward the woman. Her hands were busy with her hair and she had hairpins between her lips, but her eyes met his steadily.

"You are laboring under a slight misapprehension," Wentworth told her, smiling. "I did not put the seal upon the man's forehead. I was merely testing it to see if it were genuine. There have been forgeries, you know, attempts to hang crimes on the Spider that he didn't commit. And the Spider has served me well on occasion." He presented a card between two deft fingers. "Allow me...."

THE WOMAN thrust the last pin into her hair, patted it deftly into place and took the card. She smiled into his eyes. A curious trick of hers, always to look directly into a man's eyes.

"All right, Mr. Wentworth," she answered pleasantly, "we'll let it ride that way. I've... heard of you."

Wentworth shrugged slightly, frowned as he peered along the waterfront street they were following. The sound of the siren had died. Either the patrol had stopped, or it was no longer necessary to race at top speed and the men wished to avoid being conspicuous.

"When you see a traffic cop, stop!" Wentworth called to the taxi driver. He faced the woman again. "There is no use debating it further," he said. "You're convinced...."

"Man, I *saw* you!" she cried.

"May I point out," Wentworth said pleasantly, "that you had been knocked unconscious a few moments before? Well, skip it. Your sister, you said, was kidnaped by those men? Your baby sister, you said."

The girl's lips were too painful to smile. "I call her that," she said, her tones muffled. "She's only a few years younger than I am, but I've always looked after her. My name is Margaret Stone. Our home is in Westport...."

"Of course," Wentworth exclaimed, "I knew that combination of names was familiar. You're the daughter of Roland Stone, the artist..." The taxi jerked to a halt beside a mounted policeman. Wentworth leaned out, showing his police card. "That patrol wagon—did it pass here?"

"Turned off two blocks back, Mr. Wentworth." The mounted cop saluted respectfully. "Toward the river."

Wentworth did not have to instruct the taxi driver. He whirled in a tight U-turn, scooted back up the wide, rough street.

"I assure you," Wentworth told Margaret Stone gently, "that if I can save your sister, I will." The taxi squealed to a stop. "Stay in the taxi."

Without waiting for Margaret Stone to answer, he stepped from the cab, gave the driver money. "Wait here," he told him shortly, "and there's another five coming to you. You did a good job of trailing."

The driver winked, hit the brim of his cap with his knuckles so that it lifted to show his dust-streaked forehead.

"Mr. Wentworth, it was a pleasure!"

Wentworth was frowning as he strode back to the corner the patrol wagon had turned. Too many people had heard and remembered his name. He was tied inevitably with that shooting there on Madison Avenue and while police might not be able to prove that he had used the seal, he had no wish to start a train of investigation that might handicap his work against the kidnapers. Police suspicion had been directed toward him as the Spider before this, but had been laid to rest, he hoped, forever, when the commissioner, Kirkpatrick, had seen Wentworth and a person in the disguise of the Spider fighting side by side. Actually, it had been the woman to whom his heart was pledged, Nita van Sloan, valiantly risking her life to clear him. But police did not know that....

Wentworth turned the corner openly, sauntered along the side-street toward the river tapping his sword-cane carelessly to the pavement. The patrol wagon had just cleared the curb and was rolling slowly toward him. A warehouse door, sliding shut, marked the spot from which it had come. Tension oppressed

Wentworth's heart, but he kept his
manner casual. If anyone on the patrol
wagon remembered the appearance of
the man with the cane who had fired
on them, Wentworth was as good
as dead. A gunman could fire from
inside the van without being seen.
Wentworth's glance toward the patrol
wagon seemed to hold no particular
interest, but his keen eyes missed no
detail. He saw the man beside the
driver turn his bullet-head quickly

and say something to the pasty-faced man behind the wheel,
and both stared at him fixedly. Either he was recognized, or they
were suspicious of his prompt appearance at a danger point....
THE PATROL wagon jounced and rattled on toward the
main street and Wentworth continued his stroll, nothing in
his manner showing that he half-expected a bullet in the back.
Nevertheless, he managed to sway his body considerably from
side to side as if he swaggered and twice he deliberately stumbled. Small movements, but they would make aiming difficult.
Little things like that had saved his life more times than he
could remember.

He could not make up his mind whether the van's failure to
stop was a good omen or bad. It could halt around the corner
and the men could come back to take him from behind if he
entered the warehouse. Even a moment's hesitation in his action
might precipitate an attack. Wentworth felt the blood pump-

ing hard through his veins and a sense of exhilaration swept over him. It had not been love of battle which had inspired a younger Richard Wentworth to pledge his life to the defense of humanity against the jackals of the Underworld, but always in the conflict with a keen foeman, he felt the stir of a fighter's heart within his breast.

There was a slight smile on his lips as he turned deliberately into the office doorway of the warehouse from which the patrol wagon had just rolled! The door gave beneath his hand and from a dusty desk in a corner a man slunk to meet him, washing his hands drily before him. He was weazened, but, it seemed to Wentworth, more from cunning than from age.

"Yess," he whispered, his voice extremely sibilant, "What can I do for you, ssir?"

The light was brighter near Wentworth and he barely controlled a start as the man lifted his head and showed his eyes. They were pale, watery blue and, with a feeling of utter unreality, Wentworth recognized their almond, slanting form. *The man was part Chinese!*

"I'm from the *Herald-Tribune*," Wentworth said briskly, concealing the dismay he felt. "I saw that police patrol wagon come out of here and thought I'd find out what it was all about. Did they raid you?"

Wentworth's easy words, the brusk, keen manner he had assumed were a better disguise than make-up and wigs could have contrived. He knew many newspapermen intimately and his imitation was perfect. Beneath his calm exterior, he knew a deep sense of dismay. It was possible, of course, that this Oriental's presence here was no indication of the membership of the band which was perpetrating the kidnappings. Certainly, those fake police had been whites. But if Chinese were behind the crimes…?

Something like a shudder tugged at Wentworth's muscles. The thought of white girls kidnaped by Chinese was horrible enough, but it was memory that prompted Wentworth's consternation. He had fought Chinese before this, and his battles against them stood out terribly clear in his memory. They had been the Spider's most fearful enemies; and the death that they had visited upon the white race was a thing to make the strongest man grow pale!… Abruptly he guessed the reason for the kidnaping and his heart contracted with fury. The motive was—must be—*white slavery!* And some of the girls had been brought to this place as prisoners! It was hard for the Spider to hide his rage….

The half-caste ducked bows over his constantly washing hands. "A misstake, ssir." His words hissed like a snake. "Yess, yess, you have made a misstake! The patrol wagon iss come, yess, but it iss only that they keep ssupplies here, and they come for ssome, yess, yess!"

WENTWORTH FORCED a laugh. "That's one on me," he said cheerfully. He lifted his cane as if in farewell salute— and clubbed the man to the floor! The blow landed above the Eurasian's left ear and he crumpled without a moan. Instantly, Wentworth hurled himself to the floor beside the man's body. His breath hissed sharply between his locked teeth as he lay tensely waiting. Was the office watched by other hidden men? It seemed likely if this were a depot for white slavers… Moments dragged past, the silence of the warehouse continued. Wentworth got cautiously to his feet. He spoke and his voice held the accents of the man he had felled.

"Yess, yess, a misstake, ssir."

His reply was in his own voice. "Well, so long. Sorry to have bothered you." He closed the outside door carelessly, made shuffling sounds as he crossed back to the desk and creaked into the chair. It seemed unlikely, since there had been no interruption, that men were watching the office, but he still was not sure that someone was not listening. He did not wish to be discovered until he had made certain preparations… Minutes crept by, soundless, uninterrupted. Wentworth relaxed, smiled a little and… the phone rang!

Wentworth had to force his hand to pick up the instrument. There could be no question that he must do it.

"Yess?" he hissed.

The sounds that crackled into his ear held a sing-song intonation that made Wentworth's lips shut tightly. The Eurasian might have been accidental, a member of any ordinary gang, but this voice that rasped Mandarin dialect Chinese into his ear was confirmation of his worst fears! Fortunately, he knew a smattering of the language. The speaker was abusive, for he called the Eurasian to whom he imagined he spoke, *wang-ba*, which meant *turtle* and was basely insulting to a Chinese. The voice demanded to know if the "foreign devil" was gone. Wentworth answered with an affirmative, a hissing monosyllable, and the line went dead. For a moment after he had replaced the phone,

21

Wentworth sat staring hard-eyed at the unconscious form of the Eurasian. His fears were terribly confirmed. The criminals were Chinese! He jerked to his feet. He must snatch those kidnaped white women from their filthy hands! What a fearful thing threatened his country's people!

Wentworth moved smoothly into action, binding and gagging the Eurasian with scraps of his own soiled clothing, crossed swiftly back to the telephone. His course was plain, but before he blew this criminal stronghold to pieces with his guns, he must take certain precautions. For himself, the Spider had no fears, but he could not risk the safety of these kidnaped women if he should fail! The Spider was a mighty fighter, but no human creature could be forever invincible....

Still using the Eurasian's voice, he called the home of Nita van Sloan and when she answered, he clattered to her in pidgin English a summary of the "newspaper man's" visit. While he talked, he tapped on the mouthpiece of the phone with a finger-

Richard Wentworth

nail, tapped out an entirely different message in Morse code. Nita, heeding certain words in his greeting, would ignore what he said and jot down the Morse message of the tappings: *In ten minutes, send police to warehouse at 794 West Second Street. Kidnaped girls prisoners there.*

He doubted there was a listening tap in the wire, but it was certain that someone maintained auditory surveillance over the office, else there would have been no call about the "foreign devil." The Chinese would wonder why the Eurasian found it necessary to make the report and would investigate, but by that time... Wentworth was frowning as he tapped out the message. It was not the Spider's practice to call in police help. For one thing, it was too dangerous to himself, but those girls must be saved at any cost....

Nita replied in an impersonal sing-song. "Velly well. My send message." She hung up then and a cold circle of steel jammed into the back of Wentworth's neck! Hard hands clamped down on his shoulders!

"That's a gun, punk," a man whispered harshly. "And it's hair-trigger. If youse even wiggles your ears, it's curtains!"

CHAPTER 3
THE DRAGON'S CLAW

WENTWORTH HEARD the man's shoes squeak twice and swiveled about in the chair to face him. The man who had challenged him was the driver of the patrol wagon. He wore a police uniform with putteed legs and behind him was a second man similarly dressed except that he wore slacks.

"Come on!" the driver gestured with his gun. "Talk up!"

Wentworth rested his elbows on the chair arms and lifted his hands palm foremost. "Sure, I'll talk. I'm tickled to death that you two cops came in. I walked in to visit my old friend,

whom you see reclining gracefully on the floor, and found him like that. I called my girl friend at the newspaper office to tell her about it, and you heard me kidding her along."

"Oh yeah?"

"Oh, yes indeed!" Wentworth nodded merrily, but his gray-blue eyes, half hidden beneath shrewd lids were taking keen measure of the situation. It was apparent that the two men had not recognized him as their enemy of Madison Avenue, but their suspicions had been aroused by his presence on the warehouse street and, even as he had feared, they had parked the patrol wagon and returned.

The driver thrust his gun forward pugnaciously. "And what was this tapping business on the telephone, huh? I s'pose that was more kidding."

"Oh, no, no!" Wentworth shook his head seriously. "That's a nervous habit of mine I've been trying my best to break. It annoys the operators."

The second man stepped forward. "He's too damned wise. Let's take him to the chief."

Wentworth teetered back and forth in the swivel chair. The springs creaked protestingly. The man's words were welcome. If he would only take him to the head of the kidnaping gang... The driver pulled him out of the chair and tried to slam him against the wall. Wentworth set his muscles and the driver recoiled, stumbling from the violence of his own thrust. He shook the revolver....

"Now, don't yuh!" he howled. "Now, don't yuh do it!"

Wentworth lifted quizzical brows. "Do what, my friend?"

The second man was stooping over the telephone. Wentworth did not hear him call a number, but he was already talking in a swift undertone.

"Okay," he mumbled, "send up a boy to lead us down. I don't want to meet the *dragon's claw* in the dark."

The words had no meaning for Wentworth, but there was an awe in the voice of the man that made Wentworth's eyes narrow. Once he had fought a band of Chinese who had used the five-clawed foot of the imperial dragon as their mark, but they had been stamped out to the last member. Was it possible that those fierce slaughterers had reorganized?

The driver stepped close and jabbed his gun muzzle into Wentworth's stomach while the second man stepped behind him and found his two heavy automatics. He weighed them admiringly on his palms. "Say, this bird carries swell rods!" He slipped them into his pockets. "Thanks a lot, buddy. You won't be needing these again. You're going with us."

"You couldn't drive me away now," Wentworth assured him. "Not until I've seen *the dragon's claw!*"

A heavy blow against the base of his skull sent him reeling while pain blazed through his brain. "I told you he was a wise guy," said the cop who had taken his guns. "We'll have to tell the chief about that."

TEN MINUTES passed, then a steel panel that made a part of a side partition clicked open. Wentworth's eyes were burningly on the black opening, but even he was surprised at what he saw there. The girl was young; little more than a child she seemed, and she stood very demurely in the opening, her feet in felt slippers very close together, the pajamas of heavy peach-colored silk draping exquisitely about the curves of her slight body. Her voice was sweet, but strangely deep. It held the indefinable slurred accent of the East.

"Bring the vermin and follow me," she said.

The two false policemen stared at her respectfully. The driver thrust Wentworth forward with a gun.

"The other creature, too," the girl directed. "Untie his feet so that he can walk. Lock the door."

Wentworth studied the girl, saw that her dark, shining eyes gave him a masked scrutiny. In that single sweep of her eyes, he felt more menace than in all the rough bullying of the two men. He knew the East, none better. Many of his early years had been spent there. He knew the cruelty latent in these exquisite, small creatures and if he read her glance correctly, his identity was no secret to her. Even that fact did not add to his danger. In the moment of his discovery, his life was forfeit.

None of Wentworth's thoughts showed in his expression. His brows lifted quizzically, he swept a suave bow to the Chinese girl.

"It is truly worth associating with these specimens," he gestured toward the two men, "to have had these eyes gaze upon such beauty! The vermin is at your service." Wentworth thought he caught the hint of a smile in the black eyes.

"Yes," she said quietly, *"at-my-service."*

The driver's shoulders shuddered.

"Geez, the way she said that!" he whispered. *"Geez!"*

The Eurasian, half-conscious, was thrust ahead through the darkness, the driver walking behind him. Next came Wentworth, beside the Chinese girl, and the second man in police uniform brought up the rear with one of Wentworth's guns in each hand.

"Better keep both those guns on me," Wentworth warned gently. "They're set at hair trigger and you wouldn't want a bullet to mar the little lady here."

"Put the guns in your pockets, fool," the girl ordered softly.

The man stammered with fear.

"Honest, Ya Hsai, I was just making sure the guy didn't escape. There wasn't no gun pointed at you. Geez, if I put the guns away…" His voice broke as the girl slowly turned her head. "All right, all right, they're in my pockets, see?"

The girl's action startled Wentworth. So far as he knew, there was no weapon trained on him. It was possible that hidden men pointed guns, but it would fit with the girl's Chinese sense of humor to hold him prisoner without weapons, a prisoner only of his own imagination and the unknown. He leaned close to her, whispering.

"That was not a wise move, Ya Hsai. You are very lovely… and very near to me!"

He was sure this time that her eyes smiled, though he could see her face only dimly in the reflected light of the electric torch the leader carried. The feet of the false policemen scuffed noisily and the sounds were mighty in the high, empty vault of the warehouse. The man ahead turned.

"Hey!" he called, "how in the hell can I tell where the *claw* is?"

"You can't," replied Ya Hsai softly. "Let us hurry…."

"But, say…."

"Hurry!"

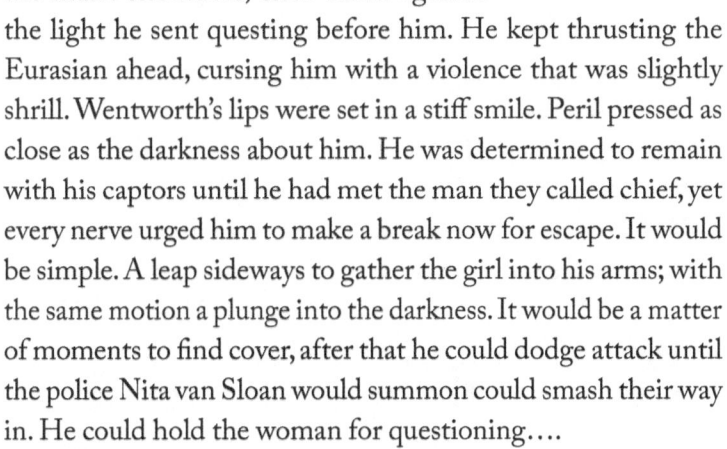

THERE WAS fear in the hunch of the man's shoulders, clear black against the light he sent questing before him. He kept thrusting the Eurasian ahead, cursing him with a violence that was slightly shrill. Wentworth's lips were set in a stiff smile. Peril pressed as close as the darkness about him. He was determined to remain with his captors until he had met the man they called chief, yet every nerve urged him to make a break now for escape. It would be simple. A leap sideways to gather the girl into his arms; with the same motion a plunge into the darkness. It would be a matter of moments to find cover, after that he could dodge attack until the police Nita van Sloan would summon could smash their way in. He could hold the woman for questioning….

As if she guessed the trend of his thoughts, the girl, Ya Hsai turned her shining eyes upon him in a curiously intent inspection. He wondered a little at her silence, her lack of coquetry. Allurement was not only the natural inheritance of the East; it was trained into their women's soft slight bodies from infancy until their whole brains glittered with facets of conscious and deliberate enticement. Yet Ya Hsai did not so much as brush her silken self against his swinging hand, nor veil her eyes from his stare.

"I think the Chief will be very pleased that you come into his presence," she said finally, the words formed carefully by her slim, pale lips, making a subtle music. "Yet I do not understand how you came to fall prisoner to these ignorant ones. Unless… unless you wished to be captured, Wentworth *san!*"

Wentworth's stiff lips twitched a little at her pronouncement of his name. It was damnably quick identification, however contrived.

"You are a reader of minds, Ya Hsai, which means that you are wise as well as lovely," he murmured softly. "Permit me to…."

Ya Hsai's hand closed sharply on his arm and she tugged him toward her. "Quickly, lift me and jump." Her voice was no more than a hissing of breath.

Wentworth was accustomed to split-second action, to movement on the reflex of sound and word without the intervening necessity of thought. His left arm encircled the girl's shoulder and he sprang past her, pivoted so that her feet were flung clear of the floor and into his arms, and swept on again with the momentum of the original movement. Behind him, men's voices blended in a scream of incredible anguish. There was the single blast of a gun and Wentworth halted, his breath coming sharply, but more from the urgency of the thing he guessed than from his brief flurry of action.

The crook's hand torch lay on the floor, its beam diffused thinly upward. Its upmost edge touched a man's dangling feet, glistened on dark drops which fell before them, that pattered on the dusty floor like heavy rain. The Eurasian was not in sight, but the second policeman, he who had fired that single shot, was stretched upon his back on the floor, his body wrenched in pain. His arms were half-drawn toward his stomach, but death had come before ever his hands touched. He had been ripped open from belly to chin.

Ya Hsai laughed softly. "Are you trying to break my ribs, Wentworth *san,* as *the dragon's claw* undoubtedly broke the ribs of yonder ignorant one?"

Wentworth became aware then that his arms were flexed hard about the body of Ya Hsai. He set her brusquely upon the floor, shook her by the shoulders.

"You deserve death," he said harshly. "Can you tell me why I should not find *the claw* in the upper darkness and throw you upon it?"

For the first time then, Wentworth saw the Chinese girl's lips move with the smile in her eyes. It was a curiously lopsided smile. "If you intended to do that," she said quietly, "you would not ask the question. Come, let us go to see the chief!"

A SHUDDER that Wentworth could scarcely suppress rippled across his shoulders. The East's callousness to horrible death was no new thing to him, but it never ceased to stir horror in his soul. Those men had died terribly, and for no reason he could discern. Probably they had failed in some minor duty... He put his hands upon the girl's wrists, started grimly back the way they had come. He could just see, far ahead, the dim yellow gleam of a night-light in the office. The girl did not resist.

"You are most unwise," she whispered. "There are more of... *the claws.*"

Wentworth checked in his tracks. God knew he was familiar

SLAVES OF THE DRAGON

Ya Hsai hurled herself against his legs

and he plunged toward the black waters!

with Chinese death-traps. They were subtly triggered and the death they afforded was not always instantaneous, nor pleasant. Vaguely, he made out the shadows of boxes stacked to right and left, forming an alleyway which well might hide death. He laughed, threw the girl's light body over his shoulder, and vaulted to the pile of boxes, made his way slowly along their tops.

"I doubt," he taunted, "that there are traps here." His words broke off and he teetered up on his toes as he saw that at this point, a cross-lane cut off further advance toward the office. He could not jump the aisle and he was certain that a deadly trap would lie concealed somewhere below him there. The Chinese well might anticipate such a trick as his and prepare for it.

Ya Hsai lay quite still. She laughed musically. "It is a problem, isn't it—to know whether to go down and risk a trap, or stay here and wait for death?"

Off there in the darkness, her laughter was echoed, though not pleasantly. After that, there was silence. Wentworth set Ya Hsai gently down upon the boxes and tied her wrists and ankles.

"Why not yield to the chiefs mercy?" she asked pleasantly. "He would welcome such a brave man with open arms." Then she laughed again, "Ah, yes, and such arms as he would open! Wentworth, *san*, they are loving arms, and...."

Her voice ceased and through the warehouse came the echo of an imperative hammering on the outer door. A man cried out indistinctly, Wentworth smiled, crouched beside his helpless prisoner.

"Ah, you have friends, Wentworth *san?*"

"Not exactly. It's the police."

As if his words had become a signal, a police whistle shrilled piercingly, then another and another, reechoing from the four sides of the warehouse, and were followed by the crash of axes on metal shutters and doors. Ya Hsai sat bolt upright. Off in the darkness, a voice cried out shrilly in Chinese:

"H sun-bu!" it screeched. "The police!" Then it added something that made no sense to Wentworth. *"Wa liang-guh ya paiu-aie!* See the three eggs of the wild dragon!"

He laid a hand on Ya Hsai's shoulder and felt the involuntary trembling of her body. "What is it?" he demanded swiftly, "What is this talk of wild dragon's eggs?"

The trembling went out of her. "It means, Wentworth *san,"* she said quietly, "that we would do well to leave here quickly."

A metal shutter ripped from its hinges and clattered to the floor. A white-beamed light danced over the cluttered piles of crates, threw great hulking shadows about. Within the building, a gun spoke thunderously, then its voice was beaten down, overwhelmed by the excited chatter of a sub-machine gun. The main door crashed in and a file of police streamed out into the storage vaults.

"Why?" Wentworth urged the girl. "Why should we leave quickly?" He could see the pale loom of her face, catch the glisten of her eyes. "When I told you to leap aside from the path of *the claw,* you did not hesitate," she said. "Why delay now? I tell you we must leave quickly."

AN OATH burst from Wentworth's lips. He flung to his feet, threw his arms high, shouting. "This building is mined! Flee for your lives! The building is mined and the fuse is lighted…!"

35

His voice broke with a groan. "Those women," he gasped. *"Those kidnaped women!* Where are they? Tell me quickly, or by God, I'll leave you here to die!"

Ya Hsai laughed up at him. "Do you think death frightens me?"

Wentworth leaned close and wound slow fingers into the black coils of her hair, drew them taut and tauter until his fingers ached from the strain. A whimper of pain was forced from the girl, but Wentworth did not relent.

"Then I will save you, Ya Hsai," he whispered, "I will save you and we will see what devices my Hindu can contrive for you. We could rip the scalp from your head a little at a time. A knife could... *alter...* your face...."

"They are gone!" the girl gasped. "As Buddha lives, they are gone!"

"You lie!"

"No, no, the truth! I swear it!" Ya Hsai's voice was quiet though strained. "Do you think the chief would destroy valuable merchandise? They left long ago in boats and we only delayed to teach a lesson to those who should follow. We already knew of what happened on Madison Avenue. *Aie!* Will you not hurry? Within minutes...."

Some police had started to leave the warehouse, but others were searching the black shadows for enemies. Something like a moan rose in Wentworth's throat. Even those who went outside would not leave, but would keep close guard about the building. An explosion...! If he could not drive the police from the warehouse, perhaps he could make them chase him to

36

safety? He discarded that plan immediately. The warehouse was surrounded. He would have no chance to burst free and lead a retreat... He snatched up the automatics he had recovered from the fake policeman's body and, crouching low, peered about him through the darkness.

"What is stored here?" he demanded. "Didn't I see some oil drums? Gasoline for your boats, wasn't it?"

Ya Hsai choked the whimper in her throat. "Oh, yes, yes! When the dragon's eggs explode, flame will wash over the floor. We shall burn alive...."

Wentworth laughed into the darkness. A slim chance, but he must take it. Swift seconds were racing by. At any heartbeat of time, the bombs might let go and this warehouse would be turned into a holocaust of slaughter. Crouching low, he began a careful shooting. Now and again his searching bullets clanged on metal and when that happened, his lips twitched in a small smile. The police returned his fire with devastating volume. Wentworth retreated, keeping to cover, dragging the girl with him. The police followed him, converging from all sides, guns lancing crimson into the darkness, tommy-guns smashing lead through the stacked crates, spilling poorly stacked crates into the aisles.

Wentworth was now leading them into deadly peril and he knew it. But presently he must make their danger very real, so that they would flee without delay. The water side of the building was not far from him. Most of the gasoline probably would be stored there. Ah! His shoulders had touched the round metal of a gasoline drum. His left arm held Ya Hsai close and, strangely, amid all that turmoil, he caught very clearly the keen, high odor of jasmine. He laughed, found the steel shutters of a window and flung them open, stared down at the black flood of the river. Police boats were crowded thick and their gun lead smashed across the shutters, powdered bricks, churned the air. Across the width of the warehouse, police were slipping forward, from crate to crate, firing as they advanced.

Ya Hsai leaned heavily against Wentworth. Her breath came in gasps. "Jump!" she cried. "Oh, jump! In two minutes, perhaps even less, the whole warehouse will be blown sky high!"

WENTWORTH DUMPED the gasoline drum to its side, with a kick sent it rolling from him, slammed bullet after bullet into its side. The impact of lead kept it moving slowly and the gasoline gurgled acridly to the floor, spreading dark, dusty pools which in the night, looked like blood. Wentworth's lips were tight against his teeth. What he was about to do would cost men's lives, he feared, but at least some would survive. If they were not routed, all would perish when the great explosion came. He sopped a handkerchief in the spilled gasoline, crouched to touch his lighter's flame. The flare was instantaneous. His hand was scorched before he could hurl the ball of fire from him. Gasoline whooshed into flame and racing fire followed the still-rolling gasoline drum. But when it reached… Wentworth sprang to the window-sill, threw his arms high, and cried out with a deep, carrying resonance.

"In God's name, leave this building! In half a minute it will be blown sky-high!"

The gasoline drum blasted, scattering gouts of flame. Another bullet-pierced drum became a flaring torch. Police began to draw back hurriedly. Two turned, ran pell-mell from the charging flames. One man leaped to a stack of crates, threw himself forward on his belly, bracing a sub-machine gun with deadly steadiness. Wentworth heard the pound of guns, the shouts of men behind him. With a shrill, frightened cry, Ya Hsai hurled her weight against his legs. Wentworth reeled, as he caught at the casement and missed, then plunged, head-over-heels, down, down! The blow of the black water was like the punch of a gigantic fist. A weight that was terrific sound slammed against his head. Wentworth felt himself being hurtled through the river at terrific speed, knew that the water was moving with him. There was a red glare that penetrated even to the depths, a heavier dazing blow. Then, his lungs bursting with the need for air, his head throbbing with congested blood, he lived a moment of struggle and agony and… blackness….

CHAPTER 4
THE DRAGON'S LAIR

G RADUALLY, WENTWORTH became aware that there was no longer a hindrance to his breathing, though there was a sobbing catch in his throat. Strange, he thought, that he was not conscious of anything strained about his throat or lungs. And yet, there was that sound… Why, a woman was weeping! He realized then that his head was pillowed in a woman's lap and that her hand was on his forehead. It must be Nita van Sloan, but how could Nita be here? She…!

He opened his eyes and the woman uttered a glad cry and he felt her lips on his forehead. There was dim, yellow light somewhere near and it made a halo of the girl's hair. It was brown as was Nita's and it held the glint of auburn. But it was long, dangling about her shoulders—and Nita's was clustered in close curls about her proud little head... Good Lord, *Margaret Stone!* He sat up abruptly.

"The Chinese girl!" he cried. "Where is she?"

Margaret Stone's hands touched his shoulders lightly. "You must rest," she said softly. "You almost drowned. We had to...."

Wentworth nodded abruptly. "Yes, I know. Artificial respiration. My sides are sore from it..." He coughed rackingly. "Still some water in my lungs. No matter. We must find that girl...."

He glanced over the black water of the river, realized that he was in a police launch. There, on the far shore, flames cast a red glare upon the water and billows of black smoke rolled toward the sky, blotting out the stars, dimming the moon. But the river's surface was unbroken. Dimly, he recalled that Ya Hsai had hurled him backward into the river just in time to save him from the guns and the explosion. Undoubtedly, she had followed, too. But her arms had been tied behind her! If she were a skillful swimmer, she could still keep afloat, but she would be helpless amid the holocaust of that explosion! His shoulders shuddered and Margaret Stone laid a blanket across his back.

"You must rest," she said softly. "You were very near death. I told police that you were in there and made them cruise the river in case you should escape from the Chinese that way. We were lucky. You were thrown right past the boat by the explosion. No, no, don't get up; you mustn't!"

Wentworth stood smiling down at her. "Don't disturb yourself," he said. "My constitution is used to being abused. I must thank

you for your help." He extended a hand, helped her to her feet and saw that the girl was abruptly confused. Her eyes would not meet his. Why, he wondered, had she bent to kiss his forehead?

"Did you find any trace of… Lucy?" she asked suddenly.

Wentworth shook his head. "The women were all removed by boats before I ever entered the warehouse. The Chinese girl I captured told me," he said. "I do promise you, though, that if it is humanly possible to save your sister, I will do it. Undoubtedly I owe you my life. Will you come with me forward? I want to speak to the police. We have to get ashore immediately."

The girl walked ahead of him, the full rounded maturity of her body silhouetted against the dim, yellow lights of the boat, her hair lovely across her shoulders. Wentworth frowned. He hoped that Margaret Stone had conceived no foolish liking for him. True, it would relieve him of any worry about her revealing that she had seen him imprint the Spider's seal… He thrust the matter abruptly from his mind. There were too many other important affairs pressing for immediate solution.

The sergeant in charge of the police boat was chuckling when Wentworth stepped up to him. "Damned clever, these Chinese, I don't think! They kind of overdid things what with fire and bombs. The fire had chased us all out before the bombs let go! Now what kind of cleverness is that?"

"Everybody get out?" Wentworth asked quietly, feeling a vast elation. It was worth the Chinese girl's death, if by it he had saved the police.

"All but two," the sergeant nodded, "and they were dumb. Dumb as hell. They waited to try to kill the lad that touched off the gasoline. Set ye ashore? Sure, I'll be more than pleased, Mr. Wentworth...."

WENTWORTH MADE his way to a telephone before taking a taxi to his apartment, ordering his comrade-in-arms through many battles, Jackson, to patrol the East River in Wentworth's speedy smaller motor cruiser and to keep a lookout for suspicious craft which might carry the kidnaped women from other warehouse hide-outs. To the world at large, Jackson was simply the superior chauffeur of a wealthy clubman bachelor, but he was much more than that. They had served together in France, Sergeant Jackson and Captain—later Major—Wentworth, and each had saved the other's life time and again. Afterward, Jackson had chosen to continue with the man whom, above all others, he had come to respect and love. Wentworth knew that he need have no further apprehensions about the assignment after turning it over to Jackson. It would be as faithfully performed as if Wentworth himself were on the job.

After giving him his orders, Wentworth telephoned Nita van Sloan and asked her to meet him at his apartment.

"Come armed," he warned her briefly, "and be extra care-

ful. Chinese are behind these mass kidnappings and I've established contact."

Nita laughed softly, her rich contralto very lovely and warm. "Thanks for calling so promptly, Dick, lover. I'll meet you in half an hour."

There was a faint smile on Wentworth's lips as the taxi sped him toward his Fifth Avenue penthouse, atop an apartment building which he had bought so that he could have control of personnel and tenancy—a man with so many enemies could not be too cautious! His thoughts were with Nita. Not a word of alarm had she uttered, nor would she. He thought sometimes that it would not be possible to carry on his relentless battles without her warm encouragement, her ready strength support-ing him. She had, of course, heard via radio of the Spider's kills on Madison Avenue, and knew that he was in the midst of peril—for always he called her as soon as any new encounter with the Underworld was to hand. It was merely protection for her, since his enemies often had tried to injure him through her.

Wentworth chose to enter his building secretly by way of the service elevator which the superintendent had discreetly avoided watching. He thought the proprietor did a great deal of secret police work and the curious characters who came and went by that service elevator were his private spies... Wentworth's butler, Jenkyns, opening the service door, took one look at him and then, his ruddy old face wrinkled with worry, hurried him to his sleeping quarters where he insisted on giving him a hot shower and an alcohol rub-down.

Jenkyns' hair was a close, crisp cap of silver—he had served Wentworth's father before him—but there was a firm strength in his hands as he kneaded the lean body of his master, marked in a dozen places by livid scar tissue, medals of his servitude. Jenkyns could never see them without pain in his pale, blue eyes. Finally, Wentworth bounded from the rubbing table, his vigor fully restored, and began to fling on his clothing.

"Miss Nita will be here for a late dinner in about fifteen minutes," he told the devoted man-servant, "I hope I don't catch you unprepared, Jenkyns?"

The old butler turned with a smile now gouging new wrinkles in his face. "Yes, Master Dick, totally unprepared."

IT WAS a little private joke between them, for Jenkyns was always prepared for any emergency. He refused to have a chef, for, in his opinion, no one save himself could prepare things properly for his master. It suited Wentworth well, for the fewer servants he had, the less chance there was that his secrets would be revealed to the world. He had only three. They knew his entire life, and they would defend him to their last breath. The third, Ram Singh, a Sikh of high birth who had dedicated himself to Wentworth, had gone now to call for Nita.

Wentworth's brow was smooth as he paced swiftly along the hallway, through the long living room whose doors were open on the terrace, and into the high-ceilinged music room. The shower and rub-down had restored him fully and his brain raced over the day, sorting out the things he had learned, probing into the mystery of the kidnappings. Almost absently, he lifted his prized Stradivarius from its case and tucked it beneath his chin, stroked its strings to soft harmony and began to play. His music—his teachers had wrung their hands in despair at his refusal to make the violin his career—was a release for him. He thought best with the strains of great masters soothing his soul....

He did not hear the door buzzer which announced Nita's arrival, but became aware of her abruptly, standing in the archway that led to the drawing-room. He did not stop his playing, but his eyes smiled and he wove the air he played subtly into another that was his love song to her. Wentworth's eyes never left her face and the sweet smile lingered on her lips. When he had finished, she came to him and held out both her slim, white hands.

"I was beginning to worry, dear," he said, drawing her into his hungry arms. "Any time Ram Singh is a moment late, there is a serious reason—and you must be at least four minutes behind schedule!"

"There *is* a serious reason," Nita now agreed. She led Wentworth into the living-room, and a huge tawny dog barked at him deeply, but did not bound toward Wentworth as he was wont to do. The Great Dane lay on the rug before the wide, stone fireplace while a boy of eight tugged at his ears and made mock of slapping his jaws.

Wentworth looked at Nita questioningly, and, her full lips compressed, she drew him back into the music-room. "His mother was kidnaped yesterday," she said. "They live alone in my building and I learned about him from the superintendent. She was stolen while he was at a play-school yesterday afternoon and he almost cried his eyes out last night, alone, without supper."

The kindliness was wiped from Wentworth's face and the hard grim lines of the fighter crept out. "That's damnable!" he said. Nita laughed ruefully. "You will wait for dinner, won't you, before starting out again?"

Wentworth bit his lips with impatience, but forced himself to calmness. Nothing was to be gained by going without food. He must harbor his strength... He whirled sharply toward the door as he heard an abrupt outcry, instantly hushed, in the servants' section of the apartment. He was in motion almost before the cry had died, springing with great bounds through the living-room, hand flashing to his lapel....

Damn it, how in the world had he happened not to holster fresh guns? It was incredible carelessness—a thing he never did when a battle was underway—to go unarmed. He checked an instant in the hallway, snatched a cane from a closet, and pelted on toward the rear of the apartment.

Dazzling light slapped him in the face. Wentworth pitched to the floor and, ahead of him, guns yammered fiercely. But even in falling, Wentworth had acted. The cane whistled through the air, crashed against the blinding light and darkness closed down on the hall. The fall became a somersault and Wentworth was charging again, close against the wall.

WENTWORTH DID not need to speculate on what had happened. He had been followed here by the men of the Dragon! Incredible as such infinite precaution might seem, the Chinese evidently had not been willing to credit his death in the explosion, but had kept watch on the police and either had seen him rescued or spotted him when he was landed. But it meant even more ominous things. The Chinese scarcely would have troubled to pursue him unless they had in some way connected him with those Spider kills on Madison Avenue!

These thoughts were a flash in his brain as he took the final leaps to place him beside the door of the kitchen, from which the guns had flamed. The lights there had been extinguished and his destruction of the flashlight had plunged the whole section of the apartment into temporary blackness. He was remembering now that Nita carried a light automatic, but he had been well on his way when he discovered that he had left off his own... Another thought twitched at his heart with pain. *Jenkyns!* Good God, what had they done to him? There could be no doubt that it was he who had cried out a few moments ago—and that cry had ended with fearful abruptness! Yet it would be fatal for Wentworth to charge through that gaping door where murder lurked. If he called a warning to Nita... but he must! He masked his mouth with his hands to disguise the direction from which his voice came.

"Stay back!" he cried. *"Assassins!"*

Nita did not answer, but the Great Dane sent his defiant deep bark down the hall. Wentworth's heart leaped. It was a chance....

"Charge, Apollo!" he cried. *"Charge!"*

A savage snarl rumbled through the darkness, then no other sound save the thud of the huge dog's racing feet. A gun cracked once into the hallway, a man cried out a guttural Chinese curse and a flashlight beam now groped through the door. Across its

47

white ray flashed a tawny shape, there was a snarl that ended in a muffled, worrying growl and was drowned in a man's cry of strangling death! Wentworth sprang through the doorway. He had no fear that the dog would mistake him in the dark for one of the enemy. Its acute sense of smell would prevent that.

Wentworth found a man's arms in the dark. Instantly his hands gripped, he heaved back, pivoted and let go and the man screamed until he hit the wall. A crunch ended his terror. It was fierce, swift work in the darkness—a man who packed death in either hand and that beast which worked in silence, but whose saber teeth tore and slew, a beast that weighed a hundred and fifty pounds and which, reared on its hind legs, would top a small man by more than two feet!

The door whipped open and a man whirled, arm rigid before him as he tried for one last shot at the killing demon. The dim light of the outer service hall was behind him and Wentworth saw him and could not dodge. He gripped a man's knife-wrist with his left hand and with his right was gouging into his throat, but his enemy was powerful. As if he sensed the thing that was happening there in the doorway, Wentworth's opponent spun on his heel, trying to swing him closer to the leveled gun.

"Gun, Apollo!" Wentworth gasped *"Gun!"*

He had trained that Great Dane, spent hours in drilling so that Nita might have his constant protection at her side. Apollo needed no urging to fight for the man who had raised him from puppyhood. His long, powerful body straightened in a lunge that took him ten feet through the air. The gun blasted, but it was a split-second too late. Apollo's teeth seized the wrist and the man screamed shrilly as the impetus of the dog's leap hurled them together to the floor in a writhing heap. He got his wrist free of the dog's jaws. Wentworth saw the man reel to his feet, saw Apollo rise from the floor in a savage leap... and the door clapped shut!

LIGHT BLAZED abruptly in the room and Nita stood, pale-faced, but determined, in the doorway, her blunt, black automatic in her right hand. She leveled it at the head of the man Wentworth fought and he dropped his knife and rolled his eyes to heaven in petition for mercy. He could not talk past the fingers that gripped his throat, and already his face was dark with congested blood, his eyes bulging. Wentworth flung him to the floor, whipped him over on his face and lashed his wrists with his own belt.

"Apollo, in the hall!" he gasped.

Nita reached the door in a bound, jerked it open, straightened slowly and let it close again. She leaned her shoulders against it, sucking in deep breaths, her head lolling back. Wentworth took her in his arms....

"It's all right," he whispered, "all right, dear. Look, Jenkyns needs your help." He led her to where Jenkyns was crumpled on the floor, half on his face, a knee drawn up acutely against his belly. There was an ugly bruise above his left ear. As Wentworth had hoped, Nita forgot the horror in the hall to minister to Jenkyns. Wentworth carried the aged servant very gently to his room, then returned to the kitchen. Two Chinese lay dead on the floor, one slain by Apollo's slashing fangs, the other crumpled against the wall where Wentworth had hurled him.

In the hall, Apollo still crouched, growling, over a third. Wentworth spoke to him sharply and the dog looked up, eyes red with battle lust. Wentworth had to speak a second time before he arose sluggishly from his prey. Abruptly, he was a puppy again, tongue lolling over blooded teeth, eyes bright with the eagerness for praise. Wentworth dropped a hand to his head, smoothed the bristling hair along his spine. Apollo rose on his hind legs, put his forepaws on his shoulders and tried to lick his face. Wentworth laughed, slapped the dog's hard ribs and led him from the room of death. Abruptly, the outer door whipped open and Wentworth whirled, fists clenching… It was Ram Singh. His eyes rolled fiercely, and there was the gleam of his teeth through his thick, bushy beard. He calmed at sight of Wentworth, and *salaaming* low, lifted cupped hands to his forehead.

"Thy servant is a miserable sluggard, *sahib*," he cried. "There was fighting and he was not here! *Wah*, thy servant is no Singh, no lion…."

Wentworth laughed softly, clapped the Sikh's broad shoulder, felt the muscles hard and eager beneath his touch. "Bemoan not, my warrior," he said softly. "There will be more work for thy knife this very night!"

There was a weary while during which police came and explanations were made and finally Wentworth faced Nita again in the drawing-room. Nita smiled faintly. "No, Dick, no dinner for me. I don't think I shall ever be able to pet Apollo again," She shuddered a little, the smile still on her lips. "Fine talk for the Spider's girl friend," she said gaily. "Come on, I'll treat to make up for it."

Despite the efforts of both of them, it was not a very gay meal. The child had fallen asleep and had been left behind with Ram Singh and Apollo on guard, though Ram Singh had protested violently that his master needed his services more than the boy did. They finished eating quickly and Wentworth sent his Hispano-Suiza roadster swiftly through the night—darkened streets to the Holland Tunnel under the Hudson River, and then toward the Newark airport.

"It is absolutely necessary that the government get on this case right away," he assured Nita. "I've already talked with Hoover of the F.B.I. over the telephone and he insists he can't do anything until the kidnapers cross a state line or use the mail—both of which they've carefully avoided. We'll use our influence, pull some wires and see if we can't get some action. You can do those things much better than I can."

NITA PUT her hand quietly on his arm. "Dick, I've sworn that you should never go into battle without me again. You're asking me to change that.... Are you sure you aren't merely sending me to Washington to get me out of danger?"

Wentworth drove over to the curb and stopped, smiling at Nita, taking both her hands in his. "I won't swear that I'm not," he said gently, "but it is damnably important that the government step into the picture."

"Don't you want me with you, Dick?"

"Always," Wentworth replied shortly, "I don't think I could carry on without you, darling, but I'm terribly afraid for you."

"The Spider afraid?" Nita mocked him.

"Yes."

His quiet monosyllable startled Nita. She bowed her head to his shoulder, not crying, not doing anything but feeling his nearness to her. Wentworth's arms closed tightly and he stared out into the darkness of the street, his eyes wide and unseeing. A man would think the hurt would die after awhile, the hurt of their barren lives. The fact that they could never be more than this to each other had been settled long, long ago. Marriage to both of them must mean the fulfillment of their love in children. Sharp laughter pushed against Wentworth's lips, but he choked it back. Could the Spider have children—the Spider upon whose shoulder the hand of the law, of disgrace, might drop heavily at any moment of the day or night? There had been moments when both of them had tried to forget that, had turned their faces toward the ultimate happiness of their dreams... Madness, utter madness.

Nita sighed softly. "I think I'll adopt that little boy, Dick. He's a nice little thing and so alone."

Wentworth could not hold back that painful laughter this time. "We'll have to hurry or you'll miss the plane," he said harshly. "Be on your guard every moment after you land, Nita. I'm not by any means sure that we've shaken off pursuit."

Their parting was casual. It was not often that either of them gave way to emotion. When the plane lifted and, gaining altitude had swung in a slow bank to southward, Wentworth went back to his roadster a little heavily... There was a deftness and a rhythm about Wentworth's driving as about all of his movements. He handled a car without belligerence, but with an easy confidence that other drivers recognized. Not even taxis challenged the smooth progress of his roadster. Tonight, he drove recklessly... At the apartment, Ram Singh was waiting in Wentworth's Daimler town car and he made the transfer without a moment's delay. For a few minutes after he entered the Daimler's tonneau, Wentworth leaned back, utterly relaxed, on the cushions, driving from his heart and brain all worry and pain. Ahead of him lay desperate peril. His mind as well as his body must be ready to meet it, else the Spider might well lose that split-second speed which had snatched him from so many deadly traps. For he was going into the heart of the enemy territory, going to Chinatown, there to seek out the lair of the Dragon!

CHAPTER 5
"THE DRAGON CALLS—"

THE SPRING night was soft with the gay voices of young people. The top decks of Fifth Avenue buses were crowded and happy couples strolled along the sidewalks. Terror had not touched them yet, though they must have felt the chill touch of apprehension at news of the wholesale kidnappings. But they could not know the things that the Spider foresaw. To him, it was apparent that the few women who had been stolen had been almost experimental, a mere hint of the things that were to come. The size of the enemy forces, the thoroughness of their preparations, the fact that they dared to pose as police, all pointed to the strength of the Dragon. No such organization as

There was a gaping wound exactly in line with the silencer
box through which Wentworth had fired!

that would have been formed for a few scattered captures. No, it was much more than that, much more fearful, more threatening....

The gay, lighted streets gave way to the shadowed squalor

of the East Side and the Daimler wove southward toward the cluttered warrens of Chinatown. The narrow streets jig-sawed through an area of less than half a square mile—and yet thousands of Orientals lived there, burrowing down into the earth, jamming into tiny rooms, living the existence of a little China in the heart of the West. Overhead, the elevated trains racketed, slamming into the junction of Chatham Square. Heavy trucks thumped and rattled past their doorsteps, all the mechanical tumult of the West, and yet they were entirely apart from it, as detached as deaf mutes from the clamor of living.

Wentworth alighted from the Daimler two blocks north of Mott Street and, his dapper clothing exchanged for less conspicuous garb from the secret wardrobe in his car, he shuffled along with drooping shoulders which totally concealed the lithe confidence of his usual stride.

A withered old Chinese sat in the dim doorway of his shop and smoked a long-stemmed pipe. Was Wentworth mistaken, or did the man's quick, beady eyes follow him piercingly as he slouched past? It was nonsense, of course, but there seemed to him to be a tenseness about the whole district. Usually the streets were a mingling of the new and the old, aged men in somber dark pajamas slippering along; young men in exaggerations of college styles, gay-banded hats upon their heads; slant-eyed children out scampering and screaming in a queer mixture of Eastern jargon and Western slang; a sightseeing crowd following a bus barker into a fake "joss house."

It seemed to Wentworth that tonight there was a dearth of the old-world men, an increased number of the young who aped the gangsters of the prohibition era—and there were no children in the street. True, it was late, but that usually mattered little. Whereas, usually, Chinese shop proprietors sat deep in the shadows of the interiors, waiting like slant-eyed spiders for customers, tonight they were in their doorways, either sitting and smoking as had been that old man Wentworth thought watched him, or merely standing idly, hand tucked into wide sleeves, blinking at nothingness. Yes, Chinatown was wide awake tonight, and that fact was somehow darkly ominous.

A black limousine rolled up before a joss-house and stopped to permit five white men to alight. They were laughing and joking among themselves, but their performance was not convincing to Wentworth. He watched them go into the Chinese temple, then strolled casually after them. A young Chinese stared at him fixedly, did not even turn his eyes when a man stopped beside him and whispered sibilantly in the Mandarin dialect.

"The Dragon calls!"

WENTWORTH GAVE no indication that he had heard, but those few words changed his plans. He had intended following those five white men into the joss-house. But it would not be necessary. It would not be easy to trail these two here in Mott Street where any white man was conspicuous, but it must be contrived. Wentworth found a taxi driver who was willing to remain parked with a passenger, with the flag of his meter up. From the darkness of the cab's rear, Wentworth kept his eyes on the two men. Though there was a great deal of movement in Chinatown this night, the small area permitted him to maintain surveillance without movement. He saw finally that one of

57

the men entered a dim shop where the curious candies of the East were vended and that, through long minutes, he did not leave again.

Wentworth paid off the taxi and returned to his Daimler. In its curtained tonneau, pressure on a concealed button caused the left half of the seat to slide smoothly forward, revolving as it moved to reveal a closely hung wardrobe in its back. Wentworth folded upward a mirror ringed in shielded neon lights, opened a tray of make-up materials and began the alteration of his face.

Under his skillful touches, the skin tautened and became sallow, shining where it drew tightly over bones. His lips vanished and his mouth was turned into a straight, thin gash. It was the work of moments then to transform the nose into a harsh, predatory beak, to gum on bushy brows and draw a long-haired wig over his head. That was all, except for a wide-brimmed slouch hat of black and a cape which flowed from his shoulders almost to his heels. When he had finished, he stared for a moment at the reflection in the mirrors, lips twisted in a slight smile. The mechanics of his make-up turned that expression into a sinister grimace. Here was the man the Underworld dreaded even above the vengeance of rival's guns, more than the entire forces of the law. Here was... the Spider!

When he glided from the car, Ram Singh stepped to the pavement also. He bowed simply, lifting his cupped hands to his forehead in his recurrent token of utmost submission.

"My master said that there would be work for his servant's knife!"

"I must go alone," Wentworth told him slowly. "Do thou

keep watch and await my signal." He described the place he planned to enter, then left the disgruntled Sikh, moving with the peculiar limp that was part of the Spider, his shoulders now twisted as if by some malignant disease. He would be glad of Ram Singh's able support in the place where he was going, but he doubted that even alone he would be able to trick his way past the guards. If it came to open battle, he would miss the keen, swift knife work of the Sikh. He shrugged his twisted shoulders. It was a chance he must take, as he had taken so many others. If he could penetrate the barriers, find the leader of this criminal conspiracy, this man who called himself the Dragon... Wentworth's thinned lips parted in an ugly smile and his hand went to the butt of one of the twin automatics that nestled beneath his arms.

As he hunched his way along Pell Street and turned into Mott around the Blood Angle where so many Chinese had died in tong wars, he kept his eyes on the confectionery shop which the man summoned by the Dragon had entered. At long, almost regular intervals, other men were going into the place and, while he watched, none emerged. Nor as Wentworth had hoped, were they all Chinese. It made his task easier that the Dragon planned to use white men in his damnable plot. But how in the name of God could white men join in such vicious crime? White men helping to kidnap women of their own race into the vile bondage of a yellow criminal! Wentworth's eyes had tightened a little as he limped toward the shop, drawing his cape's skirts more tightly about him. God grant that when retribution overtook the Dragon, it would fall to the Spider's lot to punish some of those traitors!

WITHOUT APPEARING to, Wentworth scanned minutely every inch of dim stairs and shop as he clumped heavily down past a wrinkle-faced old Chinese who seemed asleep on his high stool behind the counter. The men ahead of him had not paused, nor spoken, but gone straight ahead through the curtain of thick, dark silk which hung across the back of the narrow room. Wentworth did the same, almost strangling in the thick dust that stirred as he pushed through the drapery. Beyond, all was darkness, but he dared not show a light nor hesitate. He pushed steadily on until he was sure the sound of his footsteps had passed beyond the shopkeeper's hearing. Then he paused, pressed close against the wall of the hallway along which he had moved and waited, muffling even his breath. The very beating of his heart seemed damningly loud. He must wait here until another man entered the place, must avoid being seen or detected—and follow the other. He was too familiar with the ways of the Chinese to dare a reckless advance. The memory of those dragon claws which had slain three men in the warehouse made a cold spot in his heart. It was not fear. The Spider was no stranger to death and the risk of death. But if he should fail! He smiled slightly, He did not expect to fail....

Abruptly, his head jerked toward the shop. There was a faint thread of light as the curtain stirred, then feet slippered almost noiselessly toward him. There was little Wentworth could do to conceal himself. He hugged the wall, slipped an automatic into his right hand. If he were discovered.... The steps slowed as they neared him; the strides were long and measured, from the sound, as if a man crept upon an enemy!

Wentworth weighed the automatic on his palm, calculated his distances. He could make no error. The first blow must blot out the man's senses.... Within arm's length of Wentworth, the man had paused. His breath was sibilant, abruptly loud in the narrow area. Had he discovered the presence of an intruder, or was he...?

Ah! That whispered word! He could not be mistaken. The man was counting in Mandarin, "... *sang, liang, su, wu...* " His voice died, but Wentworth counted on deliberately in his mind, heard the man pace forward.

A slow breath was forced out through Wentworth's lips. He stepped on the spot where the man had stood and began to count, but his mind was not on the thing he did. He was visioning once more that scene in the warehouse when claws had swooped viciously from the ceiling and disemboweled three men. That trap, or something equally horrible, he had avoided here by merest chance. There could be no other interpretation upon the man's timed pause there in the hallway. Wentworth was familiar, God knew, with the torturous ingenuity of the Chinese which filled their warrens with death traps as a protection against invasion. He had penetrated them before with captor guides, and he knew their intricacy. It was clear that by standing on this precise spot, and counting to a certain sum instead of striding straight on, the man had prevented a trap from being sprung.

Wentworth finished his count, stepped boldly forward, walking without sound. He advanced a dozen paces before he real-ized that the whisper of slippers ahead had entirely ceased. Was the man standing to count again? Wentworth doubted it. Rarely were two traps avoided in the same manner. Thus if an enemy evaded one, he would not know with what method to escape the next. Either the man suspected he was followed and lay in wait with ready knife, or else he had gone into some other passageway which branched from this one. Wentworth stood still, his lips pressed hard together. This was an impossible thing he attempted. At any moment, the floor might open beneath his feet to spill him into a lethal chamber, or the ceiling might drop sudden death upon his head. He could not even retreat, for he did not know at what spot he would have to pause to avoid the trap behind him. Nothing to do but wait for another menial whom the Dragon called….

GRIMLY, WENTWORTH settled his shoulders against the wall and steeled himself to patience. Haste could wreck all his plans and bring about his death. Minutes dragged past with slow weariness, and time after time he discovered that his muscles were tense with listening. He forced himself to relax again. Making all allowances for the interminable length of minutes spent in waiting, Wentworth realized finally that he had been crouched there for well over an hour. With an invol-untary hardening of his jaw, he recognized what that meant. The Dragon must be using another entrance to his lair, because… because the Spider's invasion had been discovered!

The fact that they had not attacked proved nothing. They were torturing him with waiting, confident that in the end his Occidental impatience would make him spring one of their traps. For a moment, Wentworth fought a mad urge to dash from the place, but he mastered it resolutely. He would fall into no such ambuscade. He forced a smile to his lips and, at that, his mind found a new ease. He settled more comfortably against the wall and slept.

Wentworth took no risk in doing so. The slightest sound, the least change in the circumstances about him would snap him instantly awake—in full possession of his faculties. And he was very tired. Excitement and the strenuous activity had drained his body of energy. There is no stimulant greater than sleep, though few men could have driven their brains to rest in a predicament like the Spider's. It was partly because of his so powerful will that Wentworth was known as the Master of Men!

A voice awoke Wentworth and his eyes snapped wide on darkness; his brain conned the remembered sounds and, though he had slept when the words were spoken, he knew abruptly what they had said:

"You have waited long enough. Your masters bid you welcome to their conference."

He frowned over one phrase. *"Your Masters,"* but he could not be mistaken. That was what had been said. He rose smoothly to his feet, touched reassured hands to the butts of his automatics. It came to him now that a woman had just spoken.

"I'm in no hurry," he answered, speaking pleasantly to the darkness. "I've been needing a bit of sleep."

He could scarcely repress a start as cool, small fingers touched his wrist. "I trust you rested well?" said the woman. Wentworth caught her wrist, jerked her close against him and bound her arms to her sides in a hard embrace. Her body yielded softly. There were no weapons in her hands, nor concealed upon her. The cadences of her voice were familiar....

"Ya Hsai!" he cried softly. "I thought you had died when you pushed that chap, Wentworth, into the river. Congratulations!"

Her voice, the warmth of her breath against his throat, held laughter. "If you have quite finished with your... congratulations... shall we proceed to meet the Dragon?"

Wentworth partly released her, but he clamped an arm tightly about her waist. "A precaution," he murmured. "I have visited gentlemen like your Dragon before!"

YA HSAI laughed. "No apologies are necessary for your... precaution!" She wove a confident way through the darkness, pausing now and then to perform various delicate operations with her hands. Wentworth knew that once she rang a bell softly. At another place, she blinked a light on and off in such rapid succession that it was almost impossible to count the sequence. It seemed to Wentworth that she coded a word in Morse... *Dragon*. After fifteen minutes of such manipulations, she paused.

"On your left, you will find a small port in the wall. Fire your gun through it."

"I have heard no shots," Wentworth urged, "and many men came this way ahead of me." He was frowning. He could not see what harm could be done by the shot, but certainly it was an unusual method of avoiding a trap.

"The Dragon uses sound a great deal," Ya Hsai explained.

"You will recall I sounded a bell. The port is a soundproofed box. You know the type of silencer used on indoor pistol ranges. But I beg of you, fire in no other place. The vibrations of a shot in this hallway would…" Wentworth felt a shudder of her delicate body.

"Would what?" he queried sharply.

Ya Hsai's voice was gentle. "Under us is a pit filled with starved rats."

Wentworth's lips set grimly, his arm tightened about the girl's waist. It was not impossible that the shot would spring the trap, but it seemed unlikely that the Dragon would condemn the girl to such a death. Not that he was incapable of it, but she would scarcely sacrifice herself so willingly… With a quick movement, he thrust out a gun with his left hand, thrust it through the port he found and squeezed the trigger. Instantly, he had snatched back the automatic, but before it was fairly withdrawn from the port, lights flashed on brilliantly. It was apparent that the vibrations of the shot had caused that.

For a moment, Wentworth was blinded by the dazzling glare, but he held Ya Hsai close while his eyes swept about him. He could make out, at first, only that he was in a large, white-walled room—that the lights came from the ceiling. Then he saw that he had indeed fired through a silencer box. As his attention focused on that, he saw that the box was drawing swiftly to one side and the wall was moving with it. Then a great, rasping cry tore from his throat. He whipped free of Ya Hsai, sprang across the room the moving wall revealed.

Against the far wall, a man sagged on shackles which

spread-eagled him helplessly. There was a gaping bullet-wound in his breast from which the red blood welled—*and that wound was exactly in line with the silencer box through which Wentworth had fired!* There could be no doubt about it. His shot had stove that deadly hole through the prisoners breast, and the prisoner was—*Ram Singh!*

CHAPTER 6
"YOUR MASTERS, SPIDER!"

FIERCE ANGER burned through Wentworth's veins. He whirled about, guns flying to his hands, eyes eager to sight the enemy. Except for himself and Ram Singh, the room was empty. Ya Hsai had vanished and there was nothing to indicate which direction she had gone. The walls were blank, doorless.

The Spider spent no time in fruitless searching. Turning back to Ram Singh, he braced the unconscious Sikh against the wall and, with quick blastings of an automatic, shot away the shackles which held him. He laid Ram Singh gently on the floor, went swiftly to work on the wound. The bullet had smashed a rib, but whether it had glanced then, or pierced inward through the faithful Sikh's vitals, Wentworth could not determine. It seemed not to have penetrated the lung, for there was no blood on the bearded man's lips. Wentworth stopped the flow of blood and presently Ram Singh's eyes opened. He smiled faintly.

"Master," he whispered, "Now all is well. Thy servant fought, but...."

Wentworth silenced the Sikh, stood and began once more to inspect the room. The silencing box had vanished as quickly and as thoroughly as had Ya Hsai. The lights… Wentworth needed only a glance to know the glass which shielded them was bullet proof. He would be given no opportunity to darken the room, then. Grimly, he settled himself near Ram Singh, set his shoulders against the wall. That he was under hidden observation was apparent at once. Clearly, it did not suit his captors that he should be at his ease. Had they expected the Spider to batter himself against the impregnable walls?

In the center of the floor, a small opening appeared and Wentworth heard a sound which sent him leaping toward that small round aperture. The sound was a frantic, thin, animal squeaking. And Ya Hsai had said that, below the floor, were pits filled with the huge gray rats of China—starved to viciousness!

Wentworth slapped his hat over the opening, darted to Ram Singh's side and snatched a razor-keen knife from his girdle. As he whirled again, a shout rose to his lips. He whipped out an automatic, silencer box through which Wentworth had fired thrice with lightning rapidity. Three rats were smashed to death by heavy lead and before any more could pop up from their cellar, he had once more placed his hat over most of the hole and was sawing with the knife at the rope up which the loathsome rodents swarmed. A rat's teeth rasped fiercely on the steel and over its back another sprang at Wentworth's hand. It was as if the little beasts had intelligence enough to realize what he was trying to do and were fighting to thwart him. He beat at them while he sawed on the rope, and the rats crowded upward toward him in ever-increasing numbers, crawling over one another's backs, clustering about the rope like swarming bees. And always their thin, rasping squeaks dinned upon his ears!

Wentworth realized that he was panting, that the sweat was streaming into his eyes. The rope could not be severed, would not fall. It must have a core of steel, and the screech of knife on metal was drowned up in that filthy, ravenous chorus from below. His hands were bleeding from a score of bites. If only he had some means of permanently plugging the hole… Furiously, he pointed his automatic downward and bullet-scraped one side of the rope clear of rats. He could see some of them fall upon the writhing bodies of others he had already struck down. No end to their teeming numbers… There was weariness like a lead load in all his limbs, yet there could be no faltering. If, for seconds, he left this opening unguarded, the room would be filled with the ravenous rats and there would be no hope of escape. For a long time, he and Ram Singh might fight them off, but their numbers, the piercing wounds of their teeth would wear them down and… there would be an end. But he dared not think of that. There might be deaths more horrible than being eaten alive by rats, but none that Wentworth could think of.

In a frenzy, he shot four times down the rope, feverishly stuffed a fresh clip into the automatic. For seconds, the rats were hammered downward by lead, being torn to bits by the others.

"Master!" It was a faint whisper from Ram Singh. "Master… Thy servant is doomed. Stop the hole with his body…!"

WENTWORTH'S LIPS twitched as he tried to throw a smile toward Ram Singh. Not only for himself, but for the brave

The Dragon touched the gong and a shrill note hummed from it!

Sikh whose life was bound with his, he must triumph. He, at least, could fight and Ram Singh would lie helpless before the attack. He hacked savagely at the rope, fired three quick shots against its steel and, at last, the long line writhed down into the darkness. He scrambled panting to his feet and Ram Singh cried out a warning. From a half dozen holes scattered about the walls, great gaunt rats were leaping! Already two were tearing at the flailing arms of the helpless Hindu!

In two long strides, Wentworth reached his side and slew the rats. Then he huddled Ram Singh against the wall and, crouching beside him, began the grimmest, strangest fight for life that surely any man had ever waged. Again and again he fired, never choosing single rodents, but smashing his lead through thick-pressed groups of them. It was easiest when they tore savagely at the dead. Those who attacked him he struck at with one of Ram Singh's knives. The Sikh weakly wielded the other.

Wentworth lost all sense of time. He had been bitten in a score of places and his hands were numb from the ceaseless pounding of his guns. There was nothing in all the world but the unending hordes of rats and his own aching arms. At last, there were no more bullets left—only the smashing weight of his guns and the keen edge of the knife. A rat fastened to his thigh and he could not hammer it off. Even dead, the beast hung on. Ram Singh ripped one from his cheek and the blood seeped out through his thick heard. Suddenly Wentworth realized that there were no more rats now except a few which slunk along the walls. The holes in the floor were closed and, against the far side of the room, Ya Hsai stood demurely, her gaze upon the floor, beckoning him to come…!

A harsh Punjab curse rasped in Ram Singh's throat and his knife flashed through the air. It missed the girl's body by scant inches and quivered in the wall for a moment before it clattered to the floor.

"Curse this wound," Ram Singh screamed. "Curse this wound that has robbed me of my skill and strength. Kill her, Master! She is no woman, no human being, but a demon…!" His breath went out of him and he sagged weakly to the floor. The sound of his breathing was hoarse and terrible. "A demon!" he whispered. "A she-devil out of the pits of hell."

Wentworth holstered his useless guns, looked down at the long-bladed knife poised across his palm and his lips moved stiffly in a smile.

"I do not leave," he said clearly, "until this man you caused me to shoot is properly doctored."

The girl moved a hand carelessly and near Ram Singh a door slid open in the wall; a robed, bespectacled Chinese minced through on silent feet, stood gravely over the Hindu. When Ram Singh struck at him feebly, he merely moved his head out of the way and squatted while his coolie assistants set about stripping Ram Singh's body.

"You have earned his life," Ya Hsai's voice barely reached him. "The fight gave the Masters much amusement." She stood beside Ram Singh's impotent knife, touched the wall and opened a door. "Come!"

"On one condition," he said calmly. "I'm aware that I can

71

be killed, or forced to obey, but before that time, your master will have lost many valuable servants. The condition is that my servant shall be healed and afterward released."

The girl stood motionless beside the door and once more Wentworth marveled at her slightness, at the child-like quality of her Eastern beauty. There was no sign that she had heard. Her head, with its smooth, black cap of hair, was bowed almost as if in prayer. She lifted it abruptly, let her lips smile.

"Your petition is granted," she said softly. "Come!"

Wentworth shrugged slightly, tossed the long knife so that its point dug deeply into the floor. He glanced back toward where Ram Singh lay unconscious while the squatting surgeon labored over his wound. He was skeptical of the easily plighted faith of the Dragon, but it well suited his plans to go peaceably with this girl to interview the man who was forcing white women into slavery. He walked through the doorway and Ya Hsai moved softly beside him. The fragrance of jasmine was about her. Her garments made a faint, silken rustling....

SHE PAUSED finally, facing a blank wall, and clapped her narrow palms together softly twice, then again twice. A narrow section of the wall before them shimmered upward, its surface glittering as if with jewels. Ya Hsai's hand touched Wentworth's arm and led him into a small room whose walls were hung in canary silks. About the walls, a ring of impassive Chinese sat upon cushions. At Wentworth's right hand, there was a slightly raised portion of the floor and on that, an old man of benevolently wrinkled countenance sat, his eyes bright beads of ebony as they gazed on Wentworth. With a start, he recognized the old man who, in a doorway, had seemed so strangely to watch him pace the streets of Chinatown. The girl beside Wentworth motioned to two vacant places in the ring of seated men. With a slight, sardonic smile on his lips, the Spider sank upon the place she indicated and Ya Hsai settled herself beside, but slightly behind him, as was befitting a woman and a slave.

The Spider studied the man on the dais. The padded robe of imperial yellow which he wore draped loosely about his gaunt body and his shoulders seemed bowed by its weight. His hands were thin as Death's, the fingers tipped in exquisite nail guards of jewel-jade, of gold and ivory. He seemed inoffensive. Except for that thing which had happened back there in the Room of Rats, this might well be a meeting of a trade tong… The man on the dais swung his bony head about and for the first time Wentworth looked directly into his eyes. He had thought them black, but there was a green gleaming in their depths like emerald sparks in clear black water. And there were other, gruesome things in those depths, shadows of hell!

Steadily, Wentworth met the man's gaze and knew that his own burned with the anger and the loathing which was deep within him. The Chinese monster's withered lips smiled a little. He turned away and struck softly a tiny gong of gold and bronze that swung beside him. On the far side of the room, a man bowed three times to the floor, touching his forehead in token of utter submission. The gong sounded again and he began to talk… in perfect English, with the broad, clipped accent of a Briton!

"Everything, Highness, is ready for the raid of the theater," he said. "The advertisements state that there are seventy-five girls in the cast. There should be easily two hundred more in the audience. By midnight, all should have been delivered to the reshipment depot."

The gong silenced him and a second man kowtowed, made his report.

"Everything, Highness, is ready for the raid on the college," he said. "The enrollment is six-hundred forty-three. By midnight, all should have been delivered to the reshipment depot."

Wentworth heard the men with a feeling of utter unreality, but with a coldness in his heart that told him only too well this was all terribly real. He had no means of knowing why he was allowed to hear these plans but calmly, deliberately before him, the Orientals were recounting schemes for the capture and enslavement of hundreds of American girls, young women who would be snatched from their beds—from the midst of an evening's pleasure—into a fate which each would gladly exchange for death. Ya Hsai's hand touched his arm and he became aware that he had swayed forward, that his fists were knotted in a fury which, if it burst, would only mean his instant death. The gong had rung again....

"*Tout est pret.* Everything is ready, Highness, for the raid on the women's penitentiary," a third Chinese was reporting, speaking this time in idiomatic French. "There are more than a thousand women there. They should provide us with ample guards and, later, they can be used for… other purposes."

THE AGED man on the dais swayed gently forward and back. "It is well," he murmured. "It is very well indeed." There was nothing old or feeble about his voice. It had the clarity of a great bell with much silver in it. Once more Wentworth was conscious of the unutterable evil in the depths of the man's eyes.

"You were brought here, Wentworth *san,* and permitted to listen," he explained now, "so that you may the more greatly relish the things which I have in store for you—so that you will realize more fully the fate that lies in store for your country after… you are gone. As soon as I have the opportunity, Wentworth *san,* I shall attend to your case. Just now, there are other matters which claim my more immediate attention."

He struck the little gong and Ya Hsai touched Wentworth's arm. "Will you come with me?"

Wentworth smiled. "Why certainly!" He got slowly to his feet while he measured with veiled eyes the distance to the dais where the aged Chinese sat. Three leaping strides would take him to it. If he swung swiftly, with his body behind it, one of his automatics would crush the man's skull. Oh, the Spider would die afterward, terribly. But, that was unimportant. The monster responsible for the enslavement of the innocent women would cause the capture of hundreds, thousands more, if he were not stopped. It was up to the Spider, wasn't it, regardless of consequences?

Wentworth already had made up his mind before he started to his feet. As he straightened slowly, he went into action. One arm caught Ya Hsai to him and he went with great bounds toward the dais. He spun the girl against the nearest Chinese and spilled the man impotently to the floor. Between him and the dais there was no obstacle at all. The Dragon turned a gently smiling face as Wentworth whipped out his automatic for the single blow that would smash the skull, and....

The Dragon touched the gong and a shrill, piercing note hummed from it. The sound stabbed Wentworth's eardrums, seemed to shake his brain within his skull. The power went out of his body and his legs went watery, pitching him to the floor. His muscles tightened into knots, cramps racked him, his heart bounded against his chest walls, and that, too, was fearful pain....

Hazily, Wentworth was aware of the Dragon, leaning forward to twist his benevolent wrinkled face into a smile.

"A little invention of mine which operates upon the muscle fibers, my son, as a tuning fork causes another of the same pitch to vibrate half the width of the room away. Luckily, it was adjusted not to feeble fibers such as mine, but to the powerful muscles of your superb body... No, Wentworth *san*, I cannot deal with you now, but while I am away I would like you to dwell upon the fact that tonight nearly two thousand of your countrywomen will be bound into Oriental slavery! Ya Hsai, take the prisoner away."

Wentworth got heavily to his feet. His body was still twisted with pain and his muscles were without strength. For a moment he stood, panting, before the dais of the Dragon. His fists knotted rigidly.

"You shall die, Dragon!" he said with a voice he fought to keep soft. "You shall die, and before that, you shall suffer for each moment of pain you inflict on my countrywomen. *Remember!*"

As he turned away, the Dragon laughed. "You remember, too,

Wentworth *san*. While you are helpless, two thousand white women...."

Wentworth cursed harshly, felt Ya Hsai's hands gentle on his arm. "I told you that the Dragon did curious things with sound," she reminded him.

CHAPTER 7
TWO THOUSAND
WHITE WOMEN

AS WENTWORTH stepped out through the door that opened to Ya Hsai's touch, powerful hands closed on his arms and hurled him prone. He scored once with his feet, and once with his right hand and two men collapsed, moaning, but there were enough others to tie him hand and foot before he could accomplish more. Ya Hsai vanished and four men carried him stolidly through dim hallways that did not even echo the slippered beat of their feet. The men were naked to the waist, powerful Mongols out of North China. They did not look at the man they carried, but chattered indifferently to themselves in a dialect Wentworth could not understand. His feet were dropped abruptly and he was thrust savagely through an opening whose door was nearly a foot thick, and seated on the sill and jams of graduated steps like those of a vault. He was unable to catch himself and pitched heavily to the floor. Immediately he was snatched up and, lifted clear of the floor, he felt a noose whipped home about his wrists and the men stepped away, stood staring at him with the dark, opaque eyes of the East which, if they see

YA HSAI

at all, are entirely oblivious to what they behold. The man near-est him spat, then turned and led the way out. The door clanged solidly into its groove, a bar chunked into place and he was alone.

Across the room, a white man's voice said civilly, "Do you

THE MASTER

know of any way of getting free of this damned Chinese torture
rack?" The voice had held up very well when it started out,
but strain broke through its syllables and made it rasp chok-

ingly before it was through. Wentworth's eyes flew to the sound and saw a man hanging by his arms, as he was himself, from a wooden frame that was like the structure for a child's swing. The analogy hit Wentworth with grim force, and with a sense of utter incredulity, he studied his companion in torture.

There was a single overhead light, shielded in a niche with bullet-proof glass as the bulbs had been in the Room of the Rats. By it, he could clearly see the twisted features of the man. Younger than himself, he was taller and broader. His blond hair was clipped short over a well-shaped head and his face was meant to be good-humored. In the agony of the rack, which Wentworth was already beginning to feel, his mouth was wrenched awry, though he fought against showing his pain. He had been stripped to the waist and the muscles of his chest corded, his arms were terribly white, drained of blood. They had not stripped Wentworth. His black cape still swung from his shoulders, though his hat lay on the floor of the Room of Rats. Even his empty guns in their holsters added to his weight.

"There is a way," Wentworth said slowly. "I'll try it in a moment. I'll have to, before my arms lose all feeling. These side supports are pretty far away..." He turned his head about and peered around his up-stretched arms. He was swinging in the middle of a cross-beam that was supported on two vertical supports which in turn were braced three ways against the floor for steadiness. The torturers did not intend to permit the rack to be overturned. Wentworth peered up at his hands, which were a full six inches below the top beam. The noose was biting deep into the flesh of his wrists and the agony of suspended circulation was searing through his hands. His heart labored. He set his lips and started to work. He started to sway from side to side, lifting his feet first to the left and bending that elbow, then to the right and reversing the process. Gradually, his body began to swing. The cord cut more excruciatingly into his wrists, but he clenched his teeth and persisted. At the apex of his swing, he should be able to hook his toes around those side uprights. After that....

"God give you strength," groaned the other captive. "God give you...."

DELIBERATELY, WENTWORTH worked his body higher and higher. The frame creaked a little with his efforts, but it did not sway, and that was well. The pain in his arms was almost unbearable. The cord had broken the flesh of his wrists and warm threads of blood ran along his arms. His toe tapped an upright and breath gusted from his lungs. He had guessed right about its distance. If only now... He pumped harder, flinging himself frantically from side to side. His toes were tapping every time. Violently, he flung to the left, to the right, back to the left, and hooked at the upright with his toe. He caught, held, and the wrench almost pulled him in two. The toe slipped, and he dangled away, spinning helplessly. Desperate, he fought to maintain his momentum, worked up again to the proper momentum and stabbed out a second time with his toe. It caught behind the upright, held. He reached out cautiously, gently with his other foot, scarcely daring to breath lest that precarious hold be loosened. His leg ached with the tension he put upon it to hold that position. The other foot...! He got it in place, tugged himself forward until he could lock his feet behind the upright and hung there, panting, grinning despite the fierce burning pain of his wrists. He had won the first part of the struggle, but the hardest remained to be accomplished. Without the help of his hands, he must work his feet, his legs, up the upright to the crossbeam, pull his body up on top of it....

The slow minutes of awful pain during which he accomplished that difficult climb were almost too much for even Wentworth's brave heart. Twice he slipped and barely managed to maintain a leg grip on the wood beams, and three times he sobbed aloud with the pain of his tortured wrists, but finally he accomplished the thing he sought. He got his legs hooked over the cross-bar from which he hung and then at long last, he could take the weight off of his arms, he could let the blood flow back into the deadened members. The torment of returning circulation was almost pleasure. It was easy afterward to grip the beam and get his body on top of it, a matter of minutes to chew the bonds from his wrists. As quickly as possible, Wentworth got down from the frame and crossed to the other prisoner. He had lost consciousness. Wentworth untied his hands, slapped his cheeks until he stirred, then delayed no longer, but crossed rapidly to the door. He had seen its thickness and had heard the ponderous movements of the lock when it was fastened. Most men would have despaired to the point of not even examining the barrier, but the Spider could not give up hope.

If it had been only a matter of his own escape, he would have lain in wait for the return of the guards hoping that he and his companion could overpower them, but there was no time for that. Before the guards came for him again, the Dragon would have completed his three raids and two thousand white girls would be his helpless prisoners! No, Wentworth could not delay. He must escape now, *now* and speed the warning to police, rush to the rescue. He had just completed the examination of the door when the man he had saved spoke casually beside him.

"Faith, I think it's easier to break through the wall!"

Wentworth turned with a smile, saw with approval that the man was massaging blood back into his arms and hands and smiling at the pain.

"As soon as the power's in them," he nodded, "I'm going to shake the hand of you. It's a gone fool I thought I was."

WENTWORTH STEPPED back from the door and looked it over slowly again. "You might be right," he said quietly. "I can force that door with explosives that I carry, but it would give the alarm at the same time, and I don't see that it would profit us much. We'll try the walls. You go to the left. Tap softly."

"A hidden door, is it?"

"Not unlikely," Wentworth said quietly, "This door is the first of any kind that hasn't been hidden." A feverish impatience gripped him, but he maintained a steely control. Not by panic, or by frantic effort was a way to be found out of this prison. The memory of the Dragon's final words prodded him with fingers of panic. He tried to lose it in the concentration of listening while he struck the panels softly. Minutes crawled past as he went methodically on with the work. It was his companion who cried out finally.

"Listen," he said and tapped with his fingertips. At that spot, the wall gave out a distinctly hollow sound. Wentworth crossed striding to his side, saw the man's eyes abruptly narrow, saw him draw slowly erect.

"I say," he began quietly, "I believe—I'm quite sure—I owe my life to… the Spider!"

Wentworth stopped, facing him, not more than a yard away, and the quiet smile still managed to make his lips seem sinister.

"Not yet at any rate," he said. "We aren't safe."

The man looked at him intently, his long, solid-seeming face was very serious. Slowly, his hand lifted from his side.

"Faith, my life is my life," he said cheerfully. "I still want to shake hands with you!"

Wentworth clasped the hand warmly, but briefly, then he leaned against the wall at the spot the man had indicated and tapped it two or three times. "You're entirely right," he said. "I think you've found a door, and a thinner one than that other or it wouldn't give a hollow sound."

Wentworth stepped back and began looking for some clue to opening it. The man thrust with all his strength, but his eyes stayed on the face of the Spider.

"Heard a lot about you, old chap," he said lightly, "Never expected to run across you, actually. Didn't want to. Rather admired your work and that sort of thing and it might be…."

He broke off as there came a slight creaking from the door. He braced his legs rigidly, used his hands for additional purchase. Wentworth stared at him with narrowed eyes before he hurled his additional weight against the barrier. He doubted that they could force it in this way, but at least they could trace the edges…

Wentworth's thoughts were not really on his task. Those words of his companion had been curiously revealing, more so than the man who uttered them probably realized. He liked the Spider, yet dreaded to meet him. Only one interpretation of that. In some way, this man was connected with the forces of law, and he dreaded to meet the Spider whom he admired, for fear that duty might put them on opposite sides. If he were not a law man, why should he be a tortured prisoner of the Dragon?

THE SPIDER'S lips were grim as he stepped back and inspected the doorway. There was a barely visible outline. He scanned its edges with his fingertips, then went down on his knees to study the floor. It was curious that a sheet of paper should be lying there, a sheet of blank paper as long and narrow as ticker tape. Queer that he hadn't noticed it before. Had it just been thrust through...? His eyes tightening, he deliberately inserted it under the edge of the door and slid it along from hinge side toward the outer edge. It was purely speculation, but abruptly he jumped to his feet and watched the door swing slowly toward him. He saw then that there had been a delicate switch in the floor which the paper had touched, that there was a spring arrangement for thrusting the slip of paper into sight....

"Must have touched some invisible button or another and caused the paper to slide into view," Wentworth said quietly. "Well, here's the way to freedom. By the way, how many men has Marshall got on this job?"

Wentworth caught the involuntary jerk of the man's muscles. The blank innocence of his, "Who do you mean, Marshall? I don't get you," was additional proof. Marshall was the District

Chief of the Government forces, and this man he had saved from the Dragon was a G-man. It had been a shrewd guess, no more than that. But it was enough. Wentworth brushed aside the other's inquiry and stepped into the darkened passageway outside the door, heard it click shut behind them. He stood motionless and heard the other's breath beside him.

"What'd you mean by that question about Marshall?" he asked. "Faith, you're a strange man."

"I have my answer," Wentworth said drily, "but your secret is safe in my hands. Glad to know that Marshall is working on these kidnappings... I think our best plan is to cause an alarm and attempt to follow whoever comes, or else force them to lead us out of here," he said. "Are you familiar with Chinese traps?"

The man said slowly. "I don't care about leaving here yet. My duty is here and... There's a girl here."

"Ya Hsai?" Wentworth asked, frowning.

"A white girl," said the man. "My... fiancée."

Wentworth cursed harshly. "There's no time for personal matters," he said curtly. "I have a friend, wounded and their prisoner. If I escape, they'll vent their spleen upon him... Didn't you hear their plans for tonight?"

"I hadn't heard... any plans," the man muttered.

Wentworth told him then, swiftly, concisely. "One of us must escape and carry the warning. We don't know what school, or theater. The prison can be only Blackhart..." He cut off his words, listening, hand touching the shoulder of the man for caution. Again, he caught the sound, the slightest possible whisper of footsteps. Wentworth's lips hardened in a smile. Were they discovered?

CHAPTER 8
THE DRAGON STRIKES!

HE STRETCHED out his arms and crouched forward. His hand brushed silk and he snatched at darkness with a harsh curse.

"Silence!" he warned.

He knew that his prisoner was slight and soft in his arms and that in his nostrils was the clear, high odor of jasmine. His prisoner laughed. He cursed and spilled the shaded light of a small flash into the corridor.

"Ya Hsai!" he cried. He gripped her tightly by the arms, his eyes tightening. He spoke very slowly. "You will lead us from this place to a safe street," he said. "You will walk six feet ahead of me and you will not try to escape. Do you know why?"

Ya Hsai laughed with a white gleaming of teeth. "I know!"

It required an hour of careful meandering through torturous passages; but finally the night wind was cool and damp on Wentworth's forehead. Ya Hsai dropped back from her leading position.

"Mulberry Street is just ahead along this alley," she said. "You will be safe now."

Wentworth nodded. He stared at her curiously, and for a moment she met his eyes. Then she caught his arm in something between a caress and fear, staring beyond him into the darkness.

87

"Oh, quickly…!" Wentworth spun about, catching at the girl's arm. He missed it, detected the trick instantly, but it was too late. She had vanished into the darkness. For a moment, Wentworth stood peering into the gloom. She had escaped so easily and yet, in all that time when they had wended through the maze, she had made no attempt to evade them. Was it possible that she had wanted to…? He cut the thought short, turned sharply to the G-man.

"There's no time to waste," he announced shortly, "We must give warning at once. I'll get a cab, send it back for you." He turned and strode swiftly along the alley, his cape kiting out behind him. Already, it was near eleven o'clock, and by twelve, the minions of the Dragon had promised, the captive girls would be delivered to the "reshipment station." Wentworth broke into a run. His Daimler was blocks away. He whistled shrilly for a taxi, and when it came started it doubling toward his own car. In those few seconds, he had snatched off wig and false eyebrows, drawn the cape close about him like a coat. The time had long since past when the Spider could ride openly in a taxi in his own well-known identity.

At the first chance, he entered an all-night drugstore and put through a call for police headquarters. When the familiar, clipped accents of his friend, Stanley Kirkpatrick, came to his ears, he spoke rapidly.

"Dick Wentworth, Kirk. The Dragon plans three raids tonight, I've found out… Yes, yes, that's the kidnaper, a Chinese. I'll give you the address of one of his headquarters, but your men will have to be very careful. It's full of traps… No, no, *Listen!*" He told his friend then of the attacks on prison, college and theater that were scheduled before midnight. "A girl's college, near New York, with an enrollment of six hundred, forty-three. By God, Kirk, the Hayes School, for a bet!"

WELL WENTWORTH knew that fashionable college, situated in the wealthiest portion of Long Island with an unusually large student body for an institution of its kind... He gripped the phone hard as Kirkpatrick began to talk.

"Your warning on the prison comes too late," he said harshly. "We don't know exactly how it was managed yet, but it seems that everyone within miles of the prison must have been stricken deaf, because its gates were taken by storm, its entire complement of guards and wardens murdered. Imagine all that, and no one heard it!"

A soft girl's voice with a curious accent was whispering in Wentworth's brain, "The Dragon does some curious things with sound!"

He stammered, "My God, Kirk! I can't explain, but I think that the Dragon made sure no one could hear by deafening them in advance... I'm going now. See you later, perhaps."

Wentworth hung up and raced from the store toward his car. Beside it, Wentworth hesitated, hand on the door. Ram Singh had been taken a prisoner from this car by the Chinese. It would be strange if they had not made sure that whoever next entered it... With a curse, Wentworth snapped his hand away from the door. He had to have ammunition without delay. Through torturing seconds, he stood staring at his car. In a hidden compartment in the back of the front seat, there were extra guns, an entire carton of loaded clips, but to reach them….

Lips set in determination, Wentworth twisted the knob of the door, stood aside from the opening and whipped it wide. Then he ran to the nearest doorway and crouched inside of it, waiting. Moments passed without any untoward happening and, his lips smiling thinly, he inched back to the machine. He still could not believe that the Dragon would have left the car innocuous….

From beside the car, Wentworth threw the brilliant ray of his flashlight into the rear. A hoarse cry started from his lips and he sprang aside just in time. Through the moving beam of his light, a fine spray of liquid spread and Wentworth stood trembling. Damnable, the thing the Dragon had tried to do. Damnable…. There was no mistaking the sharp black marking of that snake that swayed inside—the first third of its body lifted into the air, its neck distended in anger. *Cobra Rhingalis!* It could spray its venom a full ten feet through the air. If it struck the eyes, at which it would be hurled with incredible accuracy, a man was blinded and, after a while of fearful agony, he would die. Only one thing had saved Wentworth. The snake thought the flashlight was an eye….

Wentworth laughed shortly, whirled from the car, his eyes questing for a weapon. A row of garbage cans stood on the curbing. It was the work of a moment to empty one of them and push the can, as large as a barrel, into the tonneau with its open end first. Wentworth kept the flashlight on and the snake struck out again and again. The deadly venom coated the light so that its beam was dimmed, fell wet and fearful on Wentworth's bare hand.... Then he jammed the can home and the snake writhed and thumped now against the metal.

Carefully then, Wentworth cleansed his hand of the deadly fluid. His signet ring was horribly discolored... He snatched open the compartment and found the carton of clips, snapped two home into the butts of his automatics, then pulled the garbage can from the car. One shot and the snake was writhing out its poisonous life on the floor. Wentworth slammed the door and ran swiftly down the street. He needed his car vitally, but it would be no good to a dead man. He had no way of knowing what other traps were set there. And there was desperate need for haste. Kirkpatrick would have warned Hayes School, but there was no telling whether he had guessed right, nor of how quickly it could be guarded against raiders....

Wentworth's greatest chance of meeting the Chinese in combat was to speed to the theater district. An attack on any theater would be immediately known, and he could reach the scene without delay. True, the police would be on hand in overwhelming numbers, but grimly, Wentworth had determined that his own hand would mete out death to the Dragon. The difficulties of the task he realized only too well. The Dragon sat safe in the center of a hideous web. The Spider would have to force him out into the open first....

Well, the first step had been taken in that direction. The warehouse had been destroyed and already Kirkpatrick's men must be invading the Chinatown hide-out. When the raiders struck at the theater, the Spider would be on hand to trail them to their next depot!

WENTWORTH HAD acquired another hat from his car and it was the Spider again who slipped through the dark side-streets of the Upper Forties a while later—a sinister figure of hunched shoulders and limping gait at whom, time and again, people stopped to stare. Broadway was gay as always, glittering with a thousand facet-points of light. Already the theaters had begun to empty their gabbling crowds into the street; taxis made an unceasing racket of roaring motors as they panted at red lights, each with a man on the running board signaling passengers, "reserving" a cab for a tip. But all of this Wentworth scarcely saw. He was remembering abruptly that the show which would be raided was one with a large feminine cast. It could mean only one of the large musicals. He began to cover ground at an amazing speed. He crowded close to the buildings sliding between the sidewalk throngs and the walls. The Winter Garden—it must be that! Impossible for one man to guard with its exits on two parallel streets. But what would happen there would be on too large a scale to escape notice.

With a curse, he saw that police had roped off an area across the sidewalks before the Winter Garden, that fire department equipment crowded the street there and ambulances were backed to the curb. The devil! Was he already too late? Wentworth broke into a run. He was frowning, remembering that once before the men of the Dragon had posed as police. Surely, they couldn't put over the deception with Kirkpatrick in the area? Nothing could be faked on that fire department equipment, either. A policeman stepped into his path. "No passage here, sir. Sorry." He stared into Wentworth's face, and his eyes widened in sudden, startled recognition. Wentworth jolted his left fist home to the man's body, a solar-plexus blow that crippled every muscle and dropped the man unconscious to the sidewalk.

"Hey!" Wentworth shouted. "This cop's passed out!"

Two other policemen ran toward him anxiously and Wentworth crossed the line, ducked into a narrow alleyway that led to the stage entrance of the theater. Overhead, the fire-escapes made a mechanical spider-web against the glow of the sky, but there was no movement there, no thickening crowd hurrying to escape. Wentworth forced a door, gazed out over the auditorium. Men and women were sprawled unconscious in their seats, the stage was a riot of colors—girl's costumes on their collapsed bodies. Policemen, firemen, internes and stretcher bearers were hurrying out the victims. Narrow-eyed, Wentworth watched them. It was natural, of course, that they should pick up the women first. No one would gainsay an interne lifting an unconscious woman into an ambulance!

With a curse, Wentworth wove a way rapidly across the theater full of stricken mortals. There was a section of seats where only men and old women remained. It confirmed his instant suspicion. Light footed, he sped along an aisle toward the doors which opened on Seventh Avenue.

"Stop!" a man shouted hoarsely. "Looters! Stop!"

A gun banged viciously, but Wentworth had already vanished. He saw that the man who had fired on him wore a police uniform. Was he a minion of the Dragon? Wentworth believed so, but he did not fire on real policemen, and he was not positive.

He crept along in the protection of the seats, heard the man's feet beat a muffled, heavy rhythm on the thick carpets.

"Looters!" he shouted. "Shoot him down!"

Outside the door, a woman was lifted into an ambulance which Wentworth saw was already jammed to the top with their unconscious bodies. The machine whirled away from the curb with the clanging of its bell and another backed swiftly into its place. Instantly, other women were lifted into it. Never, at any accident, had he seen so many ambulances. He had no doubts that they were not ambulances, but the slave vans of the Dragon!

HE COULD see the policeman's face now and a thin smile twitched the corners of Wentworth's mouth. He could not be mistaken. That bruised left eye was testimony that was irrefutable. This was one of the fake cops who had assisted in the raid on the lingerie shop, God how many years ago it seemed! This was the very man who had clubbed down Margaret Stone and been punched by the fake sergeant. Wentworth stood up straight, heard the man's frightened yelp as he flung a wild shot at the apparition in black cape and low-crowned black hat. The Spider's bullet hammered the man backward into a seat. His feet remained jutting straight upward and out in front of the theater, a police whistle piped crazily.

Other men in blue were converging swiftly on Wentworth now. An interne whipped out a revolver and blazed at him. A bullet chipped the seat under his left hand. He crouched and placed his hat atop a seat. Both automatics were in his hand now and they began a slow drumbeat of death which was like a funeral dirge.

The fake interne, shot right through the heart, stiffened on tiptoes against the wall, then pitched forward like a falling tree. His companion turned and fled, head flung back, legs pumping. Wentworth drove him head-first with a bullet through the skull, swept the aisle with bullets from alternating guns. Two minutes—two clips of bullets—after the firing had started and the auditorium of the theater was empty of movement save where the Spider was stuffing bullets into his clips. If real police were not already here, they would come at the tocsin of his heavy guns.

On swift feet, Wentworth raced for the doors. His work was not yet done. Out there on the streets, women were being loaded into ambulances which would carry them to horrible slavery. They must be stopped, or at least held until police could come. He burst into the street, bowled over a white-coated man whose criminal face belied his internship and sprang to the roof of the ambulance before the door.

"Not an ambulance moves," he shouted. "If any man moves, he dies!"

It was a tragically perilous thing he did, but there was no other way. No more helpless women must be carried away. From the seat of the next car, a man poked out a gun. He was too slow by seconds, and he died before he could fire. Wentworth had to fire twice more and once lead ripped the shoulder of his coat, and the drivers of the ambulances fled. One tried to race away, but was stopped with a bullet that pierced him from side to side. Wentworth saw then that police were almost at hand and leaped from his perilous post. He lost his balance, staggered, and found himself staring into the front seat of the ambulance to whose top he had leaped. He cursed roughly.

"I suppose," he said shortly, "that you're looking for your sister, Miss Stone?"

Margaret Stone, who was crouched in terror in the front seat, thrust herself erect and smiled eagerly.

"Oh, I am so glad you've come!" she cried. "I was on my way to you when these men captured me. Spider, I have found another hide-out of the Dragon's men!"

WENTWORTH STARED at her curiously. He had reason to be grateful to this girl. There could be no doubt that she had saved his life when he had fallen into the river, but it was definitely odd that she should be in an ambulance unharmed when other girls were unconscious prisoners. There was no time to delay, however. Police were very close.

"Where is this warehouse?" he demanded.

"I will lead you there," she offered eagerly, climbing out....

Wentworth shook his head. "There will be difficulty evading the police. Quickly, out with it!"

Margaret Stone stared at him with widening eyes. "You suspect me! You think... Oh, I don't know what you think!" She turned, tears starting to her eyes, and stumbled away toward the on-rushing ranks of police. For a moment, Wentworth considered plunging after her, but it was already too late. He ducked behind the ambulance, stole off into the darkness. Later, he would hunt up Margaret and get from her the information.

Somewhere, sending its deep, vibrant notes into the night

air, a clock bell was now striking. Subconsciously, Wentworth counted the notes.

Twelve o'clock! Then the college had already been raided! Wentworth turned wearily away from the scene of death and defeat and a taxi sped him toward his home. The radio squeaked with the news of the night—spreading the terror of the Dragon. The announcer's voice paused abruptly, then went on, more sharply, more indignantly than before.

"I have here a report that a G-man has been murdered," he said. "A man who was cruelly tortured before he was slain, and on his forehead was—*the seal of the Spider!*"

Wentworth leaned forward sharply, listening to the details of the crime, his mouth hard and straight, his eyes tightened with pain. No doubt as to what had happened. The Dragon had struck already at the enemy who had escaped, framing him for a murder which would loose the entire forces of the Federal Bureau of Investigation upon his trail, the organization of super-trained criminal hunters who had never yet failed to get their man! And usually got him dead!

First defeat, and now this frame-up by the Dragon! Surely, the night could hold no more horror for the Spider! He was wrong. When he reached his penthouse, he stared stricken into the harassed face of his butler, old Jenkyns. Jenkyns' trembling hands reached for his and he smiled, gently, in commiseration.

"Washington just called, Master Dick," he whispered brokenly. "Some Chinese men kidnaped... Miss Nita!"

CHAPTER 9
DEATH RIDES HIGH

WENTWORTH SWALLOWED stiffly, and handed Jenkyns his hat and walked past him into the drawing-room. He stood in the middle of the floor, doing nothing, thinking nothing, but feeling the knowledge of Nita's peril as a fresh and aching wound. Why had he let her go beyond his sight and protection? But he had thought she would be safer in Washington. He had been wrong, woefully wrong....

Jenkyns spoke softly behind him. "Your bath is ready, sir. Shall I layout fresh clothing or will you retire?"

Retire? Wentworth laughed shortly. "A sack suit, dark. Is there any detail about the kidnaping of... Miss Nita?" He forced his voice to remain calm, but it had a dry, uncertain sound.

"None, sir, but Mr. Kirkpatrick asked that you call."

Wentworth crossed heavily to a davenport, signed listlessly that Jenkyns was to put through the call. A portable phone was plugged in beside him and Wentworth waited, eyes unseeing. He should be used by now to the agony of counter-attack through Nita. Foe after foe had threatened her with abominable death... Kirkpatrick's voice was hurried and sharp over the wire.

"You were right on every count, Dick," he said swiftly. "It was Hayes School, but we were too late. Every girl and woman there... God, Dick, they were carried away in meat trucks like so many sides of beef; hung in rows on racks, all apparently doped and tied up while helpless. We have all this from a man who was wounded when he tried to stop the abductions. In New York, the kidnapers were all white, but at the prison and the school, they were Chinese. In God's name, Dick, what does all this mean?"

"Among other things," Wentworth said quietly, "It means death to the white race if it continues! They got Nita in Washington. God knows how. Yes, I'm going at once. I gather that none of your men was able to follow the kidnapers? Well, murder is one way of stopping pursuit and these Chinese seem quite proficient in the art. How many dead? Fifty!… No, Kirk, there's nothing you can do. As God is my witness, I don't see that there's much I can do either. Not that I'll give up fighting…."

He handed the phone to Jenkyns, and whipped about as the door buzzer sounded. The butler moved soundlessly toward the hall and Wentworth came to his feet, hand rising to an automatic. They had struck heavily at him already, these men of the Dragon. Was it possible that they were bringing the battle to his own door again? Jenkyns peered through the *camera obscura* spying apparatus which revealed the hall in detail, then flung open the door….

"Ram Singh, Master Dick! A lady and a gentleman are bringing him in…!"

So the Dragon had kept his word! Wentworth hurried forward and saw that the two who carried Ram Singh were Margaret Stone and the G-man who had escaped with him from the Dragon's lair! Jenkyns bustled to prepare a bed for the wounded Sikh, to call a doctor and Ram Singh's eyes sought his master's, beseechingly.

"Tell them, master, that this wound is nothing, that thy servant is…" His words died; his head sagged weakly. When he

99

Nita Van Sloan

was comfortably disposed, Wentworth returned to the drawing-room where the man and woman awaited him. Margaret Stone arose instantly, hurried to him, stretching out both her white hands. She was dressed as she had been a short while before at the theater, but in the brighter light, her silver gown showed rumpled and torn.

"I met Herman and Ram Singh at the door," she said. "I came to you as swiftly as I could."

WENTWORTH NODDED quietly. She was so sure that he was the Spider! He looked away from the warmth of her eyes. Women should not be so vulnerable....

"I have to thank you, sir," he told the G-man, "for bringing me my servant. I haven't been able to question him yet." It was plain that the federal agent did not recognize in him the sinister Spider who had been his companion in peril....

"Found him wounded in Mulberry Street," the man explained briefly. "He said something about some Chinese and asked to be brought here."

Margaret Stone broke in impatiently. "You waste time! You waste time! I have found a hiding place of the kidnapers!"

"Fine! "Wentworth cried. "Have you told the police?"

"No, no! They cannot help. Even the G-men can't help. Only you...."

Wentworth smiled, shook his head. "I'm afraid you have too much faith in me. And, Margaret, don't you think you might introduce me?"

The girl was impatient, but replied shortly, "This is Herman Schull, my sister's fiancé, and a federal agent."

The man grimaced, a comical expression on his big, harsh-planed face. "And it's supposed to be a secret, that last," he said.

Margaret Stone scarcely gave them a chance to shake hands. "The place I've found," she went on rapidly, "is a steamship dock on the East River. I'm positive they have a hideout there, but I was captured before I could make sure." She told him the name of the docks. "Now, don't tell police. They'd only raid it and destroy our only clue. We must keep watch and follow any men that leave there, find their real base of operations!"

"You are quite right," Wentworth agreed somberly. His lips twitched. All of his soul urged that he race to Washington to save Nita, but he could not ignore this fresh and important clue. He tried to tell himself that it might lead him more directly to Nita than the other search, but he did not believe it; he thought, too, that Margaret's opportune appearances on the scene of crimes was open to suspicion; that she might be an ally of the criminals attempting to lead him into a trap....

Schull said, "Do you mind if I use your phone? The office probably thinks I'm dead."

Wentworth nodded and Jenkyns showed him into the hall-way. Margaret crossed at once to Wentworth's side, pressed her palms against his chest.

"Why is it," she asked, hesitantly, "that I trust you so completely? Why do I know that whatever you do will be right?"

Wentworth said gently, "Nita van Sloan is my affianced."

The girl laughed softly, eyes holding his. "I am without

102

shame," she said. She slipped her arms about his neck. "Please, am I so hard to take?"

Wentworth laughed. Herman Schull from the doorway said, ruefully, "Better watch her, Wentworth, she and her sister always get her man." He came forward slowly. "I have to ask you some official questions. My assignment has been changed." He was squarely before Wentworth, his voice steady. "What do you know about the Spider? He has killed a G-man and the heat is on."

Wentworth's smile left his lips as he returned the man's gaze. "I heard that a colleague of yours had been found with the seal on his forehead," he said seriously. "Are your superiors convinced that the seal is genuine? You know that before this it has been forged."

"Defending the Spider, Wentworth?"

Wentworth met the rising challenge in the man's voice steadily. "I make rather a fetish of strict fairness," he returned. "I have worked, though not deliberately, on the same cases with the Spider a number of times. He has more than once saved my life at the risk of his own. I tell you positively that the Spider has never, and will never, raise his hand against any officer of the law!"

"And yet his seal was found on my friend's forehead! There can be no mistake." Schull was very positive. "Our files contain the record of all of the Spider's victims. We have made chemical analyses of the ink he uses and caliper measurements of his seals to the ten thousandths of an inch. There can be no doubt that this seal has been made with the Spider's private device. Do you believe he would ever let the cigarette lighter with which he imprints it out of his possession?"

WENTWORTH THOUGHT of the slim, platinum lighter in his pocket with its ink reservoir and tiny device for imprinting the seal and he repressed a faint smile. There was within him a deep admiration for the work of the government men that went to such detail in their work—and more for the Chinese Dragon who had taken such pains in copying the seal, of which the Spider himself had given samples—on dead flesh!

"Your arguments are irrefutable," he told the G-man pleasantly. "Your logic is unshakable, and yet I tell you that the Spider did not kill that man!"

Schull nodded slowly. "I'd like to believe you. My orders are to bring in the Spider, alive or dead… preferably dead!" His face was cut by harsh lines. "It will not be easy. From my observation only such work as he performs could possibly smash this kidnaping ring…" He gazed steadily into Wentworth's eyes, his lips tightened "… in time to save… Lucy Stone."

Wentworth recalled with a start of surprise that Schull had told him his fiancée had been kidnaped by the Chinese, but he had not realized until this moment that he meant Margaret's sister.

"Miss van Sloan, to whom I am engaged, has been kidnaped, too," Wentworth said quietly. "We seem to have a community of interest, G-man."

Schull thrust out his big, blunt hand. "I'm leaving," he said abruptly. "I have a report to investigate. It's not easy to hunt the Spider, knowing that if I find him, Lucy is almost certainly doomed." He laughed harshly. "Queer to say that. I never knew that word doomed could sound so… Good-night!" He strode from the room.

The door had scarcely closed behind him when the phone buzzed faintly and Jenkyns came rapidly into the room.

"Man calling for Jackson, Master Dick," he cried. "Some friend of his he…."

Wentworth hurried to the phone. "Jackson dropped me off the boat, sir," a man reported. "He sighted some Chinks carrying girls in a fast boat, heading down the East River and through Buttermilk Channel. He dropped me off in Brooklyn…."

"Anything else?" Wentworth's voice was quiet, his eyes speculative. If this were authentic, it was clever work on Jackson's part. He had been told to make his own arrangements.

"Yes, sir," the man's voice was deferential. "He said he had the light rigged." That proved it genuine!

"Good work," Wentworth exclaimed. He sped back to the drawing room, shouting to Jenkyns. He faced Margaret Stone quietly. "I will have to leave immediately," he said. "A clue to the Chinese… Would you care to remain here? There isn't time to take you home, and it would not be safe for you to travel the streets alone." He turned as Jenkyns entered. "Miss Stone is remaining here."

Jenkyns bowed from the doorway, stood aside for her exit but Margaret Stone stood before Wentworth, hands pressed tightly together, her face white.

"You are going… into battle?" she whispered.

He laughed, "I hope so!"

Margaret Stone crept nearer, deep eyes pleading. She touched his hand. "You'll… be careful?"

Wentworth bowed, and when she had gone he frowned a little. Flattering, of course, her intense interest, but he was definitely suspicious. The Dragon might count it worth the cost to betray to him a useless hideout… And before this, the enemy had used women to spy on Wentworth, knowing his gallantry. And yet, damn it, he was inclined to trust the girl!

THROUGH THE drawing room he strode, across the vaulted music-room with its magnificent piano, the locked case which contained his priceless Stradivarius. He paused beside the pipe organ which filled one entire end of the room and with his hands tapped rhythmically on the sound orifices of three pipes. The columns of air vibrated, made faint echoes of music… Wentworth stepped swiftly down the side of the room and a panel in the walnut-lined walls slid soundlessly open, revealing a small, but efficient dressing-room whose walls were racks of clothing for disguise and whose dressing-table bore the hundred different materials which, in the Spider's skilled hands, could transform him into anyone of a score of different men. He dropped on the bench, his hands already at work… Minutes later, the hunched and sinister figure of the Spider moved across the tiny dressing-room, but not toward the door by which he had entered. Under his deft fingers, another opening appeared, giving on the service steps of his penthouse. The elevator wafted him silently to the basement.

Wentworth's brain was alert with hope as he sped in a small car he kept parked nearby toward the East River. He could trust

Jackson's observation. Within a few minutes, he could vault the small seaplane which he had ordered held ready for him into the eastern sky and there should be no trouble picking up Jackson's trail, thanks to the light he had rigged… He parked the car a block away from the slip where Jackson had placed the seaplane and the shadows that moved with him were no more silent, no less conspicuous than his progress through the night-heavy streets. He reached the slip without having seen anyone, stood on the wharf edge peering at the trim lines of the ship. He found the moorings, hauled the plane in close, stepped to a pontoon, to a wing—and stared into the muzzle of a revolver!

The gunman was crouched in the ship's single cockpit. "All right, Spider," he said raspingly. "My orders are to take you, dead or alive, but preferably dead. Do you want to start something?"

"Nothing at all," Wentworth said quietly. The light was poor here, but he could not mistake the man's voice. It was Herman Schull! This plane's presence here was the "report" he had been sent to investigate. "Would you be interested to know that some of the Chinese kidnapers are carrying boatloads of women through the Sound just now, and that I was going to trail them in this plane?"

Schull's face hardened. "No," he said shortly, "that's not my job."

A hard tension was making Wentworth's blood pound through his veins. Every moment's delay was making it more and more difficult for him to locate Jackson and press the pursuit which might lead him to a camp of the Dragon. There was no help for it. The gun was held very steadily and nothing he could do would avoid its lead. But Schull would have to leave the cockpit sometime….

"Out to the end of the wing," Schull ordered shortly. He stood in the cockpit, gun ready. Wentworth kept a smile off his lips with difficulty. He was allowed to move—and motion was all that he needed! Without any warning, he dropped into the water, interposing the wing between himself and that gun. A bullet kicked through the wing, whimpered past his ear as he went beneath the surface. He heard Schull shout, saw him spring to the wing and then the blackness of the water shut out his vision. He swam beneath the surface, came up softly in the shadow of the wharf and saw Schull kneeling on the wing, leaning far over.

A MOCKING smile twisted Wentworth's lips. He drew a gun from its holster and, clinging to the wharf, took careful aim. The least thing would disturb Schull's balance… The gun blasted. Schull's left foot, the heel blown from his shoe, slewed out from under him. His arms tossed high in the air and he pitched out into space, landing flat on his back with a mighty splash. Wentworth had seen the gun arch up into the air from Schull's hand, and he was already swimming swiftly forward when the G-man hit the water. He reached a pontoon, swarmed up on it and was standing on the wing by the time Schull ceased floundering and began to look about. Wentworth cut the water with bullets, but Schull paid them no heed. He swam directly toward the plane! Wentworth laughed softly. It was his own fault for insisting that the Spider never shot officers of the law, but it took real courage, nevertheless.

"You fool!" he shouted. "Get away from those pontoons. I don't want to hurt you, but if it's necessary...."

Schull clambered on the pontoon, reached for the wing, his face gleaming whitely up at Wentworth, his lips set in a straight, harsh line. The Spider cursed. He had small doubt of his ability to overcome the man, despite his greater bulk, but a fight might wreck the fragile plane. Wentworth bent sharply forward, clouted Schull neatly behind the ear, at the same time stepping on his hand. Schull sagged down limply, but his hand could not slip out from beneath Wentworth's foot. A few strenuous seconds then to get Schull on the edge of the wharf, but finally it was done. The shots would have given the alarm, and at any moment, the night would split with the wail of a siren...Wentworth punched the starter button and the motor whirred into quick life. Without waiting for it to warm, the Spider sent the ship skittering over the river. By the time the engine was warm enough to take off, he would be well on his way after Jackson.

Ten minutes later, he lifted into the air of the eastern end of Governors Island, leaned forward to adjust the photo-electric cell with which he would pick up Jackson's trail. The cell was adjusted so that when infra-red rays were received in a certain rhythm, it would sound a small buzzer. As long as the rays continued to reach upon its telescopic eye, that buzzer would continue to sound. On the launch in which Jackson followed the kidnapers, there was a searchlight, focused straight upward, which, because of a filter over its lens, could throw out only the invisible infra-red rays. It was merely a matter, then, of cruising the night sky above any boat spotted until the electric eye registered....

It took three quarters of an hour to find Jackson's boat and when that had been done, it was a matter of moments to locate the craft he followed. According to prearranged plans, Jackson fell back to summon police help while Wentworth continued the pursuit. The boats carrying the kidnaped women were already far down the bay, pushing straight out toward the open sea. The headquarters they sought must be a steamship. Transshipment by boat was inevitable if, as he suspected, the women were to be shipped to the harems of the East. Even that, as he considered it, seemed fantastic. In the few days' activity the Chinese surely had now seized more than enough women to fill the harems of the wealthy. No, no, there was some further vicious purpose behind the raids....

Wentworth had sped on beyond the boats, seeking their goal, but he could distinguish no steamship. Whatever craft they sought could not be much further out to sea. The Spider swung back toward land. Within a half-hour, the eastern sky would be graying with dawn. Before then, the Chinese, their prisoners, would have to be out of sight. *The devil!* Were those planes, those long, low-lying ships on the surface there? There could be no mistaking the slim, long lines, the spread of the wings. They were cleverly camouflaged, but he could not be wrong. Huge, flying ships such as were being used to span the Pacific with the new mail service! Was it possible, then, that the women were to be transported by that means?

THE SPIDER'S little seaplane hovered ever lower to the

sea as he scanned the big planes. Already, the boats bearing the prisoners were drawing near. Wentworth grimly sent his ship soaring. His course was clear, but he feared it was foredoomed. His gasoline supply could not rival that of the huge ships below, even though his speed was nearly equal. How, then, could he hope to discover the goal of these transports?

Before his eyes, the instrument board flew to bits. It was as sudden as that. Wentworth did not need to look behind to know an enemy plane had settled on his tail—that bullets had destroyed his instruments. Had he not been an experienced pilot—had he not learned above the battlefields of France the meaning of that smashing panel—he would never have survived the first few seconds of fire. As it was, he kicked the rudder, wobbled the stick and *vi raged* all in one continuous swoop. He saw the attacking plane blur past him, heard the deep roar of its motor and knew that, though he might outfight the other man, he was already outclassed by the ship. He should have guessed that the enemy would not leave its valuable cargoes unguarded from the skies.

As he whirled the light seaplane in an effort to get on his assailant's tail, he glimpsed from the corner of his eyes an entire flight of pursuit planes, diving one by one from the heights. One of them was almost upon him, a second had already left its wedge, high above, and there were two more. One against five, and his plane did not have the speed to run from them!

Wentworth laughed shortly. There was only one escape, to hit the water and hit it fast! And that meant failure of all his plans, and perhaps death!

111

Even before his thoughts had framed the words, he was tumbling down in a violent tail-spin. If he could make the pilot of that second plane think that his bullets had scored... The enemy ship stuck to him. The greasy gray streak of tracers continued to rip past, and the moment was rapidly nearing when Wentworth must snatch his ship from its spin. That would be difficult enough with the heavy centrifugal pull of the spinning pontoons....

Wentworth came out of the spin army-style, reversing his controls, but the ship staggered like a drunken thing, nosed almost into a stall before he could whip it out, skipped over the surface of the water at breakneck speed. The pontoons caught too deeply. He felt the tail whip upward and had just time to slip his belt before he was hurled violently through the air. The blow of the water half-stunned him and he sank deeper and deeper, barely conscious enough to hold his breath....

When he shot finally to the surface, he had discarded shoes, coat and trousers. He rose cautiously, lest his head, breaking the waves, draw a new attack. He was conscious of an oppressive, throbbing roar and saw that the entire fleet of great clipper seaplanes was lifting from the sea, that the boats in which the Chinese had brought their human cargoes were already sunk. His tiny plane still floated half submerged and he trod water cautiously, waiting. After the planes were gone, he might make his way to the wreck. It would support him until he could get a life preserver. If he could not do that, he was almost without hope. Twenty miles from the nearest land, he would be dependent on being sighted by some fishing boat or liner's lookout—and he was not near any direct ship-lane.

Something like fear stirred in his heart for a moment, but he smiled it away. It was not in the Spider to despair. He might be able to swim twenty miles if the tide did not set against him too strenuously. The life preserver. It would, of course, become waterlogged... The clipper planes were skimming away close to the surface of the sea, but the pursuit craft still hovered near. Abruptly, one of them swept downward in a long, graceful dive. Wentworth ducked below the surface, felt a blast, a roiling of the water that tumbled him, half-stunned, to cold depths where pressure beat terribly upon his eardrums. Desperately, badly weakened, he fought upward once more, gasped the life-giving air. There was a coldness in his breast. That had been a bomb, no doubt about that. Good Lord, if they had destroyed even the wreckage of the ship so that there was no chance of getting a life preserver... Wentworth thrust himself high to peer over the surface of the sea. There wasn't a trace of the little seaplane. Even its splinters had been sunk by the bomb, and over in the East, black clouds were rising. A storm, a storm out of the East. Why, good God, he couldn't swim twenty miles through a storm! He couldn't swim five. High above him, one of the pursuit planes was stunting jubilantly. Victory, its antics spelled, and to the Spider, death....

CHAPTER 10
IN THE DRAGON'S POWER

A S WENTWORTH had urged, Nita van Sloan was on her guard every moment of the time after he put her aboard the plane for Washington, but alertness was useless against the four Chinese who, driving a car, pinned her taxi to the curb. She shot one man, then she was overpowered. The driver of the taxi made no attempt to defend her and, within seconds, she was lifted into the other car together with the man she had killed and the sedan raced back the way it had come. Five minutes later, she was in a large cabin autogiro which lifted from a field beside the road and winged southward.

Nita was thrown into the depths of despair, not alone for her own plight, but because her captivity would be used as a weapon to harass Wentworth. God knew he already had worries enough. At the exact hour when Wentworth was taking off in his plane to pursue the boatloads of kidnaped girls, Nita was landed in a section which she identified as the heart of a swamp, probably the Great Dismal on the Virginia-Carolina border. She stared about her in stunned amazement. Under the great cypress trees were built series of long, low buildings which were hemmed in by double fences ten feet high. In the runway between the fences, great savage dogs prowled, Alsatian boar hounds. A strong shudder swept her. Well she knew what these houses were: barracks for the women captured by the Dragon!

Nita was thrust roughly across the small clearing which, bordered by quagmires and sluggish streams of swamp water, served as a landing field. Even before she reached the wire fences, the 'giro had vanished into the night skies. There was a hangar for only one plane in the swamp and its doors were closed. Apparently, the ship was there. If only she could break free and reach the plane....

Nita smiled faintly at the impossibility of such a feat. She had passed through the double fences now, men with whips beating back the dogs as she crossed, and was thrust into one of the barracks. She was searched there with a thoroughness that brought the shamed blood hot to her cheeks, then allowed to walk untended into the dormitory. The place was thronged with girls. Some few slept, but most were too terrified. They stood together in whispering groups or crouched soundless in the darkness.

For a long time, Nita stood at a window, watching the East turn gray with dawn. She felt strangely drained of resistance, and she knew a despair for the man she loved. She slipped to her knees and bowed her head on her folded hands. She couldn't know that, many miles to the northward, Wentworth's wrecked plane had just been shattered by a bomb, that twenty miles from land, he was threshing, half dazed in waters that were whipped by a rising storm. But her heart cried out to him through the gray dawn....

It was late in the morning before food was brought to the women, great buckets of rice mixed with a liberal quantity of meat. Nita read a forlorn message in the savory food. The Chinese wanted their prisoners kept in good condition for... for the fate that was in store for them! Just before noon, Nita

"So the Spider is dead? Then, Dragon, the dead has returned to life!"

was summoned by one of the women who kept guard over them to leave the barracks and go to the headquarters hut across the landing field. She was sickeningly aware of the eyes of men that followed her as she walked. If she could, she would have gladly stripped herself of feminine graces and hidden the beauty of her face!

The man whom Wentworth knew as the Dragon received her in a room which, despite the crude exterior of the building, held all the luxurious beauty the East loved. The Dragon was comfortably seated on a low divan, the live will of his eyes belying the wrinkled age of his face. Through a long minute, he inspected Nita without speech, those black, limpid eyes surveying every inch of her body. Finally, he nodded slightly, spoke in his clear, precise English:

"I really should compliment Wentworth *san* upon his good taste," he said lightly. "Too bad that he shall be deprived the sight and the beauty of you forever!"

NITA SMILED slightly, calming the pounding fear in her heart. She said quietly, "I prefer the barracks to your presence."

The Dragon chuckled, a cracked sound, curiously menacing. "I wish you to know what lies in store for you," he said gently, "So that you may the better savor your present existence. Do you know what Mongols are, my dear?"

Nita met the Dragon's bright gaze without the least wavering of her eyes. She knew the Mongols, of course, powerful uncivilized brutes from the North of China, even filthier than the Chinese coolie. Most of them lived by banditry and raiding as their Tartar ancestors had before them.

"Yes, yes," the Dragon chuckled, "I perceive that you do. Splendid physical specimens, are they not? A bit lacking in mental power perhaps. That is what a certain country wishes to remedy."

Nita stared at the man blankly. What horror was this Chinese monster hinting? A wild terror prodded her breast.

"I'm afraid I don't understand," she said and made her voice, by an effort, merely polite.

"Ah, but you will, my pretty one!" chuckled the Dragon. "I am being paid so much a head to bring American women, undoubtedly the most intelligent in the world, to mate with the Mongols of Manchukuo. Thus will a certain nation breed powerful and brainy men-children for its future slaves and wars. You understand now, don't you, my dear? You are to become the mother of half-breed slaves who will labor and fight for their dear mother—or should I say father?—country. I trust I make myself quite clear?"

Nita knew that all the blood had drained from her face. Her brain felt numb and a cold horror gripped her in a paralysis she could not break. God, yes, she understood now what this monster meant, knew terribly the fate in store for herself and these other helpless women. Slavery she had foreseen, but a slavery beneath men who were little more than beasts—to produce unnumbered children who would be slaves, cannon fodder... Nita fought for control, but knew that she staggered before the full realization of her fate. The Dragon was talking, complacently, gently:

"You need have no fears for your health, either now or later," he said. "The Mongols will be selected for physique and health. They will be allowed the privileges of the women's camp as special rewards for good behavior, and the women will have the best of medical attention. If any should kill themselves—" the Dragon leaned forward—*"their bodies will be given to the soldiers! Afterwards, the dogs will eat them.* I am aware that, after death, you could not suffer from these things, but you revere your bodies, you Westerners, do you not? Even after death, you do not wish...."

Nita pressed knuckles into her mouth, ground her lips against her teeth. In a while, she could raise her head.

"For these things," she said clearly, "Your country and this other sponsoring country will be wiped off the face of the earth. All the nations of the world will unite...."

"Ah, quite," the Dragon murmured, "but there is this aspect of the thing to consider. All over the world, we will go to gather our slave-mothers. Such a war could not be won in a day, and within a few years—the man power of the west will be exhausted. There will be no new sources of supply!"

Nita had no memory of her return to the barracks, but she knew presently that the captive girls stood about her in thick-crowded ranks, calling to her, begging to know what lay in store for them. Nita looked beyond them to the guards who kept watch. There were many eunuchs, but there were women also, white women with hardened faces who still wore the uniforms of the prisons from which they had come. What hope did they have to escape with those guards ever among them, with the barrier of the fences and the dogs, and beyond that, the trackless wastes of the swamp? She bowed her head and told them with heavy words what the Dragon had said, but she did not tell them what would happen if they killed themselves. After they were dead, they would not know, and it could not harm them. Perhaps death would be better.... Girls sank to the floor, weeping, or screamed and beat against the prison walls that held them captive....

THE DAY passed in a dull agony for Nita. When night fell, the hum of autogiro motors filled the night. Fresh groups of girls were landed and whipped into the stockades by Chinese who gloated in the pain they inflicted, who took delight in ripping the clothing from their victims with the lash. Other groups of girls were cut out of those in the barracks and herded out to be loaded into the planes and carried away. Their destination was a steamer, they learned, which would bear them to the Orient. One woman broke free of the guards and ran into the propeller of a plane. Her skull was crushed instantly, and, as the Dragon had threatened, her body was turned over to the Chinese. There were no more suicides during that night of horror... As fast as the new arrivals were settled in the barracks, doctors made slow rounds of the buildings, examining them, making typhoid and paratyphoid vaccinations, smallpox, diphtheria. It was plain the Dragon intended to take no chances on the health of his prisoners. Nita saw seven girls condemned by the physicians and separated from the new arrivals. She heard them scream, saw them slain one by one with a knife and saw their bodies thrown into the swamp.

No woman in the camp slept that night and when morning

came, they still stood about in stricken, white-faced groups. Nita saw that the eunuchs had entirely disappeared and that only women guarded them. How could any woman, however hardened, stand by and see her sex thus doomed? Nita made her way slowly across the crowded room until she faced the two guards who stood beside the door, coiled, long-lashed whips in their hands.

"Do you know what the Chinese intend to do with these women?" she asked quietly.

One of the women laughed jeeringly, but the other was as white-faced as the prisoners. Nita turned to her.

"How can you bear," she almost whispered, "to keep these women prisoners like this when you know that they are going to be made slaves of men who are nothing but savages and beasts? How can you…?"

Her voice broke in a gasp of agony, for the white-faced woman had abruptly struck with her whip. The lash cut across Nita's throat and breasts, hurled her backward with its impact and pain. After that single gasp, Nita let herself show no evidence that the whip had hurt. She smiled tightly into the woman's face.

"Have you found out," she asked, "what the Chinese are going to do with *you* when this is over?"

The woman sprang forward, lashing furiously, and the doors whipped open and more women ran in, whirling their whips, cutting on all sides with the lash. Screams and panicked cries filled the low-roofed barracks. Nita let a lash knock her to the floor and when the woman guard stood over her, striking at other girls, Nita reached out and caught her foot, spilled her heavily to the floor. Before the woman could rise, Nita snatched the whip. A blow with its heavy butt stunned the guard and Nita whirled the club about her head, gripping the slender end of the lash.

"Follow me!" she cried. "Follow me to escape and freedom!" OTHER GUARDS shrank back at the sight of Nita's determined, set face, but two more of them fell beneath the savage blows of the loaded butt before they would retreat. The prisoners stopped their frantic flight and turned to watch Nita. And suddenly their spirit changed. They crept upon the guards who had lashed them.

"Follow me!" Nita shouted again. Catching the whip handle up short, she rushed the four remaining woman guards. A lash cut her side, ripped her dress, but she paid it no heed. She seized the whip that had struck her and hit out heavily with her own. The woman fell and Nita had another whip. She flung it to another of the prisoners. The remaining guards fled and through the opened door, Nita led her victorious horde. A half-dozen of them were armed with whips now and it was the work of moments to unfasten the doors of other barracks and lead still other scores of girls to the attack.

Toward the gates, Nita raced, swinging the whip about her head. A eunuch stood inside the fence. He had a rifle with a bayonet and he ran toward them, jabbing threateningly with the keen blade. Nita flung her laughter into his face. She was without fear, swept along by the tide of battle. Who was she to fear this weakling who was neither man nor woman? She was the Spider's mate!

123

She knocked the bayonet aside with the butt of her whip, whirled the lash viciously with a continuation of the same movement. The knot cut the eunuch's face, blinded him and Nita had the rifle. She had no need to shoot the man. He ran, screaming shrilly as a woman, hands held to his bleeding face. Nita tucked the whip into her waist and, gripping the rifle in competent hands, ran on. The gate was locked, but two blows with the butt smashed it. A huge Alsatian, larger than her own Great Dane, Apollo, leaped for Nita's throat and she whipped the point of the bayonet across its neck. With a snarling howl, the bleeding dog fled and the next three were met with whirling lashes.

They were outside the stockade—*they were free!*

A half-dozen men, gripping rifles, darted out of the hut in which she had confronted the Dragon and Nita threw herself prone on the ground. She thanked God now that the Spider had made her drill so relentlessly with rifle and revolver. She had only five bullets in the clip, doubtless, and there were six men. But if she got a man with each bullet... Calmly as on a target range, Nita opened fire. Her first bullet nailed a man against the front of the hut, drove him half through a window and he lay there, writhing, for seconds, before his body, relaxing in death, slid to the ground. Nita had already fired a second and a third time and two more of the men were dead.

They had thrown themselves prone also, and their wild bullets cut among the close-crowded ranks of the women. They screamed, but their charge did not check. An avenging horde, they swept across the narrow field, Nita advancing with them. Five of the men were dead and her rifle was empty, but the sixth had fled into the hut. A joyous strength was in Nita's soul. She caught up a fresh rifle from the ground and more women seized the others, tore ammunition from the belts of the dead. With them at her back, Nita charged into the hut and… it was empty!

Behind her, she caught panicky chatter of a machine gun and she tore back through the ranks of the women she led to seek out the danger. Atop one of the barracks which she had not been able to reach and empty, a machine gun was mounted. Lying half behind the peak, the operator was apparently not yet trying to hit the women, merely to frighten them into submission. Nita smiled grimly. She doubted that the machine gun would be turned on them unless the orders came from the Dragon himself. These women were valuable property, worth five hundred dollars a head in Manchukuo!

Nita rested her rifle against the edge of the doorway and her second shot stilled the machine gun, tumbled the man who operated it lifeless to the ground. She saw then something she knew instantly she should have prevented. The autogiro was rolling out of its hangar, motor already roaring, rotors rapidly whirling. Unless she stopped it instantly… Even while the thought raced through her mind, the autogiro lifted from the ground and a thing that glittered like glass streaked down to the earth. Before it struck, Nita guessed its purpose.

"Bomb!" she shouted. *"Bomb! Scatter!"*

THE BOMB burst with a strangely small explosion and clouds of greenish yellow gas rolled upward. From its path, girls flew shrieking, without order or thought except escape from the stuff that caused excruciating pain in their eyes and turned their nostrils inside out. Quickly, Nita rallied the women nearest her and led them through the hut and out into the depths of the swamp. A few more bombs dropped, but the thick branches of trees protected them. Slowly, the escaping women made progress.

Death was all about them in the swamp. Huge brown cottonmouth moccasins slithered off into the water and two girls stumbled into quagmires and were barely snatched clear in time. For an hour, they pushed laboriously on, Nita feeling the way through a morass of stinking pools and deadly sinks. Solid ground was rare and it was necessary to climb upon the high roots, the "knees," of cypress and jump from one precarious hold to another. Only the horror behind them served to drive the women ahead. Time lost all meaning. Here, beneath the trees, was a perpetual twilight that changed little between day and night.

How much later it was, Nita could not tell, but she heard the whirring of an airplane motor and ahead she could spot a clearer space that might be an island in the swamp. Without other warning, a voice thundered down upon them: "Nita van Sloan!" it cried. "A message for Nita van Sloan."

Nita recognized the source of the voice readily enough—a loudspeaker attachment on an airplane which magnified a man's voice a million times.

"Nita van Sloan, Nita van Sloan!" it shouted again. "The Dragon knows the Spider's identity and can prove it. A little matter of tracing the ink of the seal to a certain party. It has been done. You will march to the clearing ahead and surrender there to the Dragon or the government shall hear what we know! The seal has been found on a dead G-man's forehead!"

Nita stood motionless, staring up at the green roof above her, through which the voice cried out, saying again and again this damnable threat against Dick Wentworth. She knew what they meant well enough. Dick used a special tattooing ink in his seal. If they could trace its purchase to him, prove by chemical analysis that the ink he had bought and that in the Spider seal were identical....

Nita bowed her head, and ploughed on, moving now through ankle-deep mud. A woman just behind her reached out to touch her shoulder.

"He's talking to you, isn't he?" she asked. "What is he talking about?"

Nita smiled faintly. "He's threatening to frame the man I love for murder."

The woman gasped. She was no older than Nita. Her face bore the ugly red welt of a whip, her golden hair streamed about her shoulders, she smiled, but it was a twisted mirth.

"What are you going to do?"

Nita turned wearily forward and pushed on. She was leading away from the field that lay ahead, circling it far to the right.

"What can I do?" she asked heavily. She knew what Dick would do, with his high disregard of personal considerations in the face of danger. There would be no hesitation at all, as there could be none for her. One man's life against the slavery of all these women? Bitter laughter pushed up into Nita's throat, and she bit her lips to hold it down lest it bring sobs and tears. Overhead, the voice kept on and on with its threat against the Spider. Nita's head sagged forward.

She knew in her heart that nothing she could do would prevent the Dragon from using his knowledge against the Spider, so she told herself, but those words that hammered down from above beat into her brain.

"Surrender, with those you lead, and the government shall never know the secret of the Spider!"

THE SOBS pushed out and she crushed her hands against her mouth. Oh, she knew what Dick would do and the thought of it made her very humble, but she was a woman, a woman who loved… She whirled about, reached out for the woman who followed her.

"For God's sake, tie me!" she cried. "Tie me and gag me or I… or I will surrender!"

The line of march stopped and Nita could see the white glisten of faces far through the twilight. She could see the pitying smile on the face of the woman just behind her. Nita caught the woman's shoulders.

"Tie me," she begged, "Tie and gag me, or I'll sacrifice you all for… for him."

The woman put her arms about Nita's shoulders. "What does it matter?" she asked quietly. "We are lost in the swamp. There isn't a chance in a thousand that any of us will get out alive. Those men in the plane could bomb us out of existence, and they will if they're forced to do it to prevent our escape. If we go back, perhaps the Spider or some one else will come to our rescue in time."

Nita clung to her for a moment, then she stood erect again. "I'll surrender alone," she said quietly. "That will have to satisfy the Dragon. I can say you wouldn't follow me, and you really wouldn't, you know. Why should you go back into that hell for my sake—for the sake of one man I love?"

Nita turned and ran off, stumbling, into the darkness, fleeing toward the clearing which showed as a lighter patch in the twilight head. Twice she slipped off the narrow trail of safety she had found, and twice dragged herself back by a supreme exertion of strength. That voice pounding down upon her seemed to bat panic sounds about inside the tight box of her skull.

"Dick!" she gasped. "Dick, lover!"

His name gave her strength. She ran on. Oh, it was a cowardly thing she was doing, she told herself. She was abandoning those women, helpless in the swamp. Without her leadership, what chance would they have to escape? They were all young, mere girls. What did they know of peril and death and disaster? But she knew. The Spider's mate knew. Dick would shame her with this even while he held her close in his arms, Nita knew. If ever she found his loving arms again! But God, how could she condemn Dick! She would be doing it if she failed to surrender, to stop the Dragon's revelation of evidence....

The clearing was just ahead now. Nita stood very still, clinging to the knees of a giant cypress, her lips twisted bitterly. Ahead, there lay slavery and unspeakable horror, but possibly the saving of her lover's life. Behind her, lay travail and death also, perhaps, but death free of slavery, and the possibility that some might survive. Nita threw her arms to the skies.

"Dick!" she cried. "Oh, Dick, help me to be strong. Help me to do the right thing...."

Her head sagged. She felt the burning of tears in her eyes. Slowly, she turned about. Her course was clear. From somewhere inside of her, she drew the strength to turn. She lifted her head, her eyes clearing.

"Thank you, Dick," she whispered. Foolish to think he could have heard her; foolish to talk to thin air this way. "Thank you, Dick. I have the strength... now!"

SHE PLOUGHED through the mud toward the women she led and abruptly she was aware of them not ten feet from her, following doggedly in the tracks she had made when she sought to desert them....

"Go back! Go back!" she cried. "The Dragon's men are ahead. We'll have to go around." Her voice was vigorous. She angled off to the right of the trail and a man stepped out from behind a cypress and a whip cracked across her shoulders. She bit down a scream and tried to charge him, but the whip cut her legs out from under her, spilled her, writhing, in the mud. All about her, she could hear the cracking of other whips... There was bitterness in Nita's soul. It was her weakness that had led the women into this trap, her weakness and no other cause....

Back again in the camp where the whips of the guards had driven them, Nita was half-dragged, half-beaten into the presence of the Dragon. He sat serenely on his dais as before, smiling at her.

"A brave try, my dear," he said gently. "I will see that you receive your full punishment in Manchukuo. A little I must deliver to you now…" He paused, studying her. Nita lifted her head proudly, gave him back look for look. Her moment of weakness had left her. She would not tremble before this man, nor would his punishment stir her. She laughed defiantly.

"Do you think I fear you?"

The Dragon shook his head gently. "No, my dear, but before one thing you must bow… Death. At dawn this morning, my dear, five of my planes shot down the Spider. He drowned in New York Bay, twenty miles from land." He chuckled gently. "You see, you will punish yourself. For your own selfish reasons, you led those women back into captivity. And you realize now that it was for nothing! Catch her there, fools, do you want her to injure herself when she falls? No, no, don't harm her at all. She will suffer more if you don't harm her at all. Take her back to the compound."

The Dragon chuckled drily. "There are no further obstacles. This woman's will is broken, and the Spider… is dead!"

Nita, prone upon the floor, heard the man's voice dimly, and an inarticulate protest welled up within her. Dick could not, could not be dead, and her will… It would be a sword to destroy this man. She thrust her weary body up from the floor and a glad cry sprang from her lips.

A lithe man in cape and black slouch hat stepped over the sill of a window, a gun in each hand. He laughed, and the sound was flat and strangely sinister in the small room.

"So the Spider is dead?" he said softly. "Then, Dragon, the dead has returned to life again!" He leveled an automatic at the Dragon's chest and squeezed the trigger!

CHAPTER 11
THE SPIDER IS TRAPPED!

E VEN AS Wentworth squeezed the trigger of his auto-matic, two things happened simultaneously which completely changed his plans. A man standing beside the Dragon hurled himself bodily into the path of the bullet and another Chinese, slim-bladed knife in hand, hurled himself at Nita's back. Wentworth twisted. Both guns spoke together. The combined impact of the lead hurled the knife-man bodily aside. His point was embedded in the floor; Nita scrambled to her feet.

Only then could the Spider whirl back to the leader. A man writhed on the floor, his spine shattered by Wentworth's lead but the Dragon himself had vanished! Instantly, Wentworth was embroiled in a frantic battle for his and Nita's lives. There had been six men in the room. Two lay dead. Four others snatched out guns, and knives and hurled themselves to the attack. Wentworth's twin guns spoke twice in quick, rhythmic cadence—and the four were dead. Nita threw herself into his arms.

"Dick, Dick!" she panted. "Oh, lover, they said that you were dead!"

Wentworth laughed shortly. "Damn near was, girl. Come, I must find that rat and kill him." He delayed only an instant, to imprint his seal upon the forehead of a dead man. Then he ducked back out of the window by which he had entered, taking Nita with him.

"The autogiro in that hangar!" Nita gasped.

Wentworth shook his head. "I crippled that fifteen minutes

ago. He won't get away." He was back on the fringe of the swamp, circling rapidly toward the hangar. "I knew he'd go for that if he escaped my first attack."

Abruptly, a machine gun began to chatter, its bullets rattling through the woods, dropping a gentle rain of leaves and twigs upon them. But the stream of bullets swept on and Wentworth knew the assailants were shooting blindly. He reached the hangar, which except for two dead men, was empty. Their heads had been sliced from their shoulders.

"Guards," Wentworth whispered. "They paid for letting me disable the ship." He led the way inside, keeping between Nita and the slaughtered men. "I can fix the 'giro in two minutes. We'll clear out of here and they'll be all prisoners until more planes arrive. Before that time, we'll interfere. If they try to slaughter these girls…" Wentworth's jaw shut rigidly. He got a foot on the step of the 'giro, swung up. The door pushed open hard against his chest, hurled him to the floor and before he could recover, or grab for a gun, a man stood over him with a ready revolver, the harsh planes of his face twisted into ugly lines.

"Schull!" Wentworth cried, laughing crazily. When he got to his feet he was calm again. But Schull's presence had been a shock. "You G-men believe in getting your man regardless of who suffers, don't you? Come on, let's get away from here."

Schull shook his angular head. "Not a chance. The G-men will be here in planes in a few hours…."

"What makes you think so?" Wentworth asked curiously.

"If *you* can find the place," he said slowly. "Then…."

Wentworth moved his shoulders impatiently. "You can't be

sufficiently stupid to think that," he replied shortly. "Listen, I can fix this plane within two minutes and we'll run it out of here. You can hold me hostage while Miss van Sloan goes for help."

Schull stood unmoving, his face hard. Wentworth knew it would be suicide to attempt to wrest the gun from him. These G-men could shoot. The gabble of Chinese voices came swiftly toward them. In the barracks, women were beginning a frightened screaming.

INSIDE OF the plane, Wentworth glimpsed movement and he almost cried out a warning to the man who held him at gun point. He choked down the words. It seemed cowardly to permit a Chinese to strike down a white man from behind, yet in allowing him to attack Schull, Wentworth saw his only chance for liberty—for the salvation of the thousands of prisoners here. The Chinese coming toward the hangar must be mechanics sent to repair the 'giro. Whatever happened must be soon, soon… If those Chinese arrived and gave the alarm….

Abruptly, Schull staggered forward, his hat driven down over his eyes. It was ludicrous, for the attack had been made with the cushion from a seat, and the person who had struck the G-man… Surprise at the sight of the woman almost robbed Wentworth of his chance to strike. For it was Margaret Stone who had slugged Schull! Utter amazement held Wentworth silent for moments while Schull ripped the hat from his eyes, whirled to shoot… Just in time, Wentworth lunged forward. His left hand struck aside the gun, his right went wrist deep in Schull's belly. A left and a right with rocking shoulders completed Schull's vanquishment. He slumped forward on his face and Wentworth snatched him up, tossed him limply into the plane and sprang for the engine. It was a work of instants to transpose the two ignition wires he had switched. He laughed aloud, whirled toward Nita.

"A few moments now," he said gaily. "We'll crash the lines, then you can drop me overboard to hold the Dragon in check while you fly for help…" He caught Nita in his arms in his exuberance, swung her from the ground and sprang toward the plane, dropped his lips to her hair, and… He stopped dead, staring into the muzzle of the gun which Margaret Stone leveled. Hatred twisted her face.

"You're in the way, Margaret," he called gaily, ignoring the fury. "Hop into the plane, and…."

Margaret said tonelessly, "Stay where you are. We aren't going anywhere."

All of Wentworth's doubts and suspicions of the girl flooded back upon him.

He took another step forward, conscious of Nita's arm tightening about his neck. "Don't, Dick," she whispered. He understood that she wanted to stand and let go with one arm so that she stood beside him, his other arm still about her waist. The gabble of Chinese voices was very near. Within seconds, the men would enter the hangar, and then….

"Quickly, Margaret!" Wentworth cried. "Those men are almost here. They'll kill us all!" He started forward and the gun thrust forward an inch. He could see the determination in the girl's full, young face and realized shockingly that she would shoot!

"You can go," she said, in the same dead voice, "but the woman doesn't."

Quietly, Nita took Dick's arm from about her waist, pressed her hand on his shoulder. "Go, Dick," she said calmly. "Hurry. I'll keep the Dragon and his men here. You go for help...."

Wentworth's words poured out. "Listen, Margaret, there are two thousand girls here and among them is your own sister. You know that what Nita proposes is useless. She would be overwhelmed immediately. It is work for men and Nita must go to summon help. There is no other way it can be done."

Margaret said, "If you come a step closer, I'll shoot Nita!"

Behind them, a man cried out in shrill Chinese. Wentworth whirled, his back to Margaret, and shucked his guns. He fired in swift rhythm and the three men who had showed themselves, fell writhing in death to the ground. There was more shouting, crackling orders, and Wentworth knew that a larger force of men was coming. They would overwhelm them in moments, and all chance would be lost of escape—of saving these doomed girls. He whirled desperately. This one woman could not stand in the path of these other thousands for whatever reasons motivated her. She could not. The Spider had never shot a woman, but....

HE WHEELED to face her, guns in his hands. "Damn it, Margaret," he said fiercely, "you put down that gun and help us to escape, or...."

Her eyes stopped him, her eyes that were wide and pleading. "You can escape," she whispered, "if you go with me. But that woman stays behind!"

Wentworth stared at her in amazement. Why, this was ridic-

136

ulous. Was this madness inspired by her infatuation for him, which he had suspected before?

He spoke very slowly, forcing himself to calmness. "If you force me to do this thing, there will be nothing but hatred in my heart for you. I will do it, because I hold the safety of the many above everything on earth, including my own life. But you will pay to me for the thing, and...."

He sprang forward, hand reaching for the revolver. Margaret winced back, squeezed the trigger. Wentworth felt the blow and the burn of the lead in his thigh, but even heavy bullets could not stop the impetus of his leap. He got the gun, wrested it from her and stood through long seconds staring into her face. It was white and her eyes strained wide.

"I shot you," she whimpered. "I *shot* you!"

Wentworth whirled to Nita. "Get the plane out of here. Get help as quickly as possible. An army base at Langley Field is your best bet. It shouldn't be more than an hour's flight from here at the most. There may be a radio in the 'giro."

Nita came toward him swiftly. "You are hurt, Dick. She shot you...."

Wentworth said, coldly, "Into the plane, Nita. For God's sake...!"

He sprang to one side of her and his guns blasted, convulsed in his hands. A man screamed thinly, a rifle's whip-crack sliced through the air and then was silent. Wentworth leaned against the side of the hangar; the muscles hot with pain in his thigh, weakness throbbing through him.

"Hurry!" he shouted.

Nita's voice came thin as steel. "Get into that plane, damn you, Margaret! This is your fault, and…" A hand hit flesh flatly. A woman gasped and the door of the plane clapped shut. Wentworth laughed, flung himself prone and stuffed fresh bullets into his gun clips. For the moment, the way was clear for the plane. If Nita shot out of the hangar at once she… The starter whine broke with the roar of the powerful engine. The slipstream made little whirlpools of air against the wall where Wentworth crouched. A rifleman flung himself to the ground and aimed at the ship. A single bullet finished him. Then the plane rolled slowly forward under the drag of its propeller. The hangar door was wide and Nita had set the rotors swinging above the 'giro. When she got to the door, she would be ready to jump the ship into the air….

FROM HER high perch at the controls, Nita showed her white face for a moment. There was a wan smile on her lips. She waved and Wentworth gestured jauntily with a gun in reply, then the autogiro rolled clear. Thank God, she had taken his orders without quibbling. If she had delayed two minutes longer before flying away, she would not have been able to make it. As it was, the machine guns on the roofs….

At the thought, Wentworth raced to the door and peered cautiously outside. Two machine guns on the roofs, both firing, a long line of riflemen on their knees.

He sprang clear of the door and his two guns stammered in his hands, sweeping the machine guns. Men clutched at their throats and pitched to the ground, others were hurled backward into oblivion with the solid impact of lead on bone, another slumped over the gun. They were out of the battle, but the riflemen... A bullet slashed wood splinters from the door frame into his face. His wounded leg flew from under him and a broken, shrill shouting rose from the ranks. Some were firing at the plane, others trained their long guns on him. And Nita did a daring thing. She made no attempt to lift the plane to safety, but, just above the ground, she swung the 'giro in a swift murderous charge on the rifle line!

Men threw down their rifles and fled. The dangling wheels struck others to the earth. The propeller tip smashed a head. Wentworth reached the doorpost and dragged himself to his feet. Nita must not see him down. She would not continue her flight and she must, she *must* reach Langley Field and help. If there were a radio, an hour and a half would bring help. If there were no radio, it would be more than two hours. She must land at Langley Field, convince the officials, two planes must be assembled....

Wentworth swung an arm in salute and, braced against the wall, stumbled inside the hangar. He must build a barricade of some sort to withstand rifle bullets; he must stand off the Chinese through hours while help came, and prevent Chinese planes from landing.

He ripped his clothing to bind the wound in his thigh, a double wound now, but no bone had been broken and there had not been time to lose much blood. The pain was excruciating, weakening in its intensity, but the Spider could give that no heed... Nita's plane had vanished behind the close-growing trees. Two hours and a half....

Only desultory attacks were made upon Wentworth. The interest of the Dragon had centered in the escaping plane and, if he worried about the enemy penned in the hangar, he gave no sign of it. An hour passed and Wentworth was beginning to hope. No attempt had been made to kill any of the girls, nor had any Chinese planes showed in the sky. His wound's pain had subsided to a steady throbbing. Abruptly, Wentworth became aware that his name was being shouted.

He listened to the message that was cried to him and as he listened, the color drained from his face and his mouth became a fierce and menacing line. When the man had finished, Wentworth peered carefully out at the open quadrangle among the barracks and saw that the man had spoken the truth. Nita, Margaret and Schull were captives and Nita had been spread-eagled upon the ground, her ankles and wrists tied to four stakes. There was a line of coolie soldiers, standing, grinning down at her. As he watched, guns spoke thunderously and lead crashed into the hangar from four sides.

"Will you surrender?" cried the voice that had summoned him. "If you surrender, I promise the woman shall have a clean, swift death. Otherwise…" The threat of the line of coolies was sufficient.

CHAPTER 12
THE DRAGON'S CLAWS

WENTWORTH GOT heavily to his feet, using a board he had broken from a crate as a crutch. He limped slowly out into the open. He had no fear that he would be shot down. At any time during the previous hour, a concerted attack would have killed him in that way. The Dragon wanted him a prisoner, wanted him to die slowly and by incredible tortures. Slowly, Wentworth moved out into the open.

Finally, without having seen the Dragon, he stood beside Nita. She smiled bravely up at him. "I'm sorry, Dick," she said quietly. "A bullet cut an oil line, and when we were forced down, Schull and Margaret insisted on coming back for you instead of going on to get help. We were captured within fifteen minutes after we crashed." Her lips twisted. "There was no radio...."

She was deliberately telling him that all hope was dead, now while he still held guns in his hands. Her eyes were brave. Wentworth shook his head slowly. He dropped his guns on the earth and Chinese men seized him and rushed him, without regard for his wound, to a small, concrete room that had no windows and only one steel door. Nita, Margaret and Schull were hurled into the cell with him, and a Chinese surgeon came to dress Wentworth's wound. Nita shuddered at the implication of the doctor's presence. The Dragon wanted Wentworth to be strong, so that he would live long under the torture! Wentworth glanced toward Schull.

Schull was frowning. He held out his hands. "I'm all the sorts of fool you can call me," he said simply. "But I had my job and I've tried to do it as I see fit. I was ordered to bring you in, not to save kidnaped girls. I had to do my job first, and not let personal interests...."

Wentworth smiled at him wearily, "You leaned over back-

141

wards to do your duty, Schull," he said quietly. "I can't blame you." His arm tightened about Nita's waist. "Don't worry about me, Nita. There's still a chance, I suppose, that someone followed the same reasoning I used to find you. If you are saved, don't mourn for me. Schull does an even more worthy work than mine, for he stays within the law."

Schull looked at him heavily. "I'm afraid she's going to have to answer to the law for helping you," he said. "That man, Wentworth, has kept pretty much out of this fight. I know you know each other, but I can't prove Wentworth knows who you are." He nodded toward Nita. "That makes it pretty plain you're tied up together... Guess the knowledge won't do me any good. We won't get out of here, unless someone does what you did. How did you find this place?"

"Partly luck," Wentworth said slowly. "I knew that they used planes. You probably guessed that, Schull, after you saw me use a plane on East River. You were waiting when I came ashore, I guess. Why did you follow, instead of attacking?"

"No gun," Schull told him grimly. "I lost mine overboard, and you had help. You moved so fast, I didn't have time to call a cop, or get a gun until we got down here. By that time, I began to think maybe you had a tie-up with some other crooks and it would be a good idea to corral them, too. So I followed. But you haven't said how you got here."

Wentworth paused a moment. His ears were keenly attuned. There were a half dozen guards outside, keeping up a constant, two-way patrol about the concrete cell. So far, no Chinese plane had come.

"Miss van Sloan was kidnaped," he said, "and because Wentworth had a hand in the fight against the Chinese, I figured that it would be the same gang that took her. I knew which way the car that kidnaped her went—the taxi driver told that—and I knew the Chinese used a plane. I finally found an airport, a small, private field, where Chinese had been and in a hangar there where their 'giro was stored, I found some dark, rich mud. Geologists in Washington said that mud came from either the Everglades or the Great Dismal Swamp. People living on the edges of the swamp had seen 'giros at night, and, in a village, I ran into Ya Hsai, forced her to lead me here. A man I had helping me was wounded on the edge of the swamp, not badly, but he can't go for help...."

"You lost me in the swamp villages," Schull admitted, "but your mission was pretty obvious, by that time. I used your methods except that I explored with a plane and then came here by boat."

THE CONVERSATION died. Wentworth was listening again. The camp was growing quieter. There was nothing to do, except wait for the Dragon to summon them for death, take his chances then.

Nita sighed softly. "Ah, Dick, there must be a way out. They can't kill you." She said it with gentle irony. "They told me you were already dead and you came."

Wentworth touched his lips to her hair. "I was dead," he whispered, "or almost. They shot me down twenty miles from shore, and but for a lucky accident I would have drowned. It wasn't an accident entirely, either, but Jackson's loyalty. I had him following the boats. When I spotted them, I sent him back to give the alarm to police. He met a patrol boat, then turned back and decided to back me up. He picked me up about an hour after the plane went down...."

All too soon, the steel door of their prison was yanked open and leveled, bayonetted rifles covered them while an officer ordered them to come out. With Nita's help, Wentworth limped from the cell. Margaret ran up to assist....

"Forgive me," she whispered. "Oh, forgive me, I know that this is my fault. All of it. All of it!"

Wentworth smiled. "Don't be too harsh on yourself," he said. "All of us make mistakes, and sometimes they are fatal."

Schull swore dully as they marched across the quadrangle, cursing the gleeful blows the Chinese rained upon him. Wentworth and Nita walked silently and ever his eyes quested about, seeking some escape, some chance against the overwhelming odds. There was none... They were taken to the hut, where the Dragon sat on the raised dais. There were a dozen Chinese, big-bodied men armed with heavy swords and automatics, standing about the walls.

Biting her lips, Nita hung back at the threshold. A Chinese struck her on the mouth with the back of his hand. Wentworth planted his foot in the man's back and hurtled him to the floor. Two other men leaped forward and seized Wentworth. The Chinese he had felled sprang to his feet with a knife in his fist. A quiet word from the Dragon checked him.

"No, no," said the Dragon, still chortling. "You must not use the knife, my child. We have other, much more pleasant plans for the Spider."

Wentworth turned his eyes contemptuously away, smiled toward Nita. He caught a signal in her eyes, was aware an instant later that a small, soft hand had touched his, that a knife and a gun had been placed in his fists! It was not Nita; she was too far away. And then Wentworth remembered. *Ya Hsai!* The Chinese girl stepped past his side, turned and laughed up into his face. She slapped him and then winked slowly, tauntingly, moved over and stood on the other side of the Dragon. Wentworth bowed slowly to her.

"Thank you, Ya Hsai," he called. "It's a real pleasure to see you again."

HE LAUGHED, trying to fight down his exuberance. The odds were tremendous against him, but he was armed, *armed!* He glanced about, with seeming casualness, but actually was locating the various killers in his mind.

Wentworth laughed sharply, joyously. With a backward heave, be wrenched his arms free of the two men who held him. He swung knife and gun powerfully forward and the two guards died, one with a knife through his throat, the other with the back of his skull crushed.

Wentworth flung himself to the floor behind the rampart of their bodies and began shooting. The Dragon was hidden behind a quickly closed human shield. His men had flung themselves forward to protect him and Wentworth hurled his bullets into their brains, blowing them from his path. He heard Nita cry out loudly, fiercely, and saw that she had snatched up a dead man's revolver. She imitated the Spider's strategy and used a man's body for a shield.

Then abruptly she screamed. The sound was piercing, terrible amid battle moans. Wentworth jerked toward her, thinking she was hurt and she was pointing, her eyes widened with horror, above Wentworth. She snapped her gun and it clicked emptily. Wentworth rolled, knew as he did so that he was too late. The knife was already streaking down toward him. The man's face was distorted with hate. Even a shot would not turn that knife in time. It was death....

Between Wentworth and that knife, something flashed with the speed of a bullet. A woman screamed and Wentworth had a confused idea that he had cried out in a strange voice.

There was a wild fear in his heart. Who had taken the knife in his stead and cried out in a woman's voice? God, had Nita made that sacrifice? He flung a swift, fierce look about the room. Men lay in tortured heaps, dead, and on the dais, the Dragon was sprawled on his back with a knife through his throat. Beside him, kneeled Ya Hsai. She pulled the knife from his wound and plunged it into the man's breast. Again—Again! Her face was distorted with fury. More men were coming at a run and Nita stood ready at a window, waiting for them, gun in hand. She flung him a twisted smile. Then—then the woman who had saved him...?

Wentworth dropped down on his knees and caught up the body of... *Margaret Stone.*

She was not dead, but the whiteness of her face and the fierce pumping of blood from the wound told that her life's thread was snapped. She smiled gloriously.

"Least... I could do," she panted. "I... betrayed... you."

Wentworth pillowed the girl's head in his arms, feeling pity shake him. He had not blamed this girl for what she had done. He lifted his head, tears stinging his eyes.

Schull was frantic by the window, "The planes!" he shouted. "The Chinese are here in planes!"

Wentworth was ready for that emergency. "Gasoline in the hangar!" he shouted. "Nita, free Schull. Schull, pour the gasoline over the field and touch it off. Keep feeding it slowly from the drums. They can't land in fire. They can't even fly over it. Hurry, Schull...!"

Schull stared at him, at the girl dying in his arms. His lips pressed hard.

"Quick, Schull," Wentworth hurled at him. "If you don't hurry, none of us will live, and it won't do a dead man any good to know he stuck by his duty to the foolish end!"

Schull laughed suddenly. "Okay, Spider, you win!" He went out of the hut at a dead run. The attack had eased. The Chinese were waiting for the reinforcements....

"Nita," Wentworth called. "Nita, go free the girls from the barracks. You'll find guns. Arm them and we can hold off these planes forever. There must be a radio somewhere here. Call Washington...."

NITA CAME swiftly to his side, rested a hand on his shoulder.

"Don't worry about me," Wentworth said. "It will be easy, in the confusion, to throw off this disguise and say that the Dragon was holding me prisoner. The Spider ran into the swamp."

He was conscious then that Ya Hsai had come toward them. She was smiling joyously. Her silken robe was ruined with the blood of the Dragon.

"I shall disappear into the swamp, too," she said happily. "I have a plane hidden. You wonder at me? There is no need. That man was a traitor to his country and mine. If he had succeeded here in America, a certain nation would have wiped China from the map! While I live…" There was a passionate, almost a holy, devotion in her small, childlike face… "While I live, China shall remain free!"

She ran from the hut and Nita still hesitated beside Wentworth. The hot flame of gasoline licked up from the field. Through the window Wentworth could see Schull rapidly spilling fresh drums of fuel. He stopped, ran to a stockade, began to open gates and doors….

Margaret lifted a feeble hand to Wentworth's cheek. "I'm sorry," she whispered. "Sorry… Dick! You don't… love me… at all…?"

Over her head, Wentworth's eyes met Nita's. This fight was over for them all, but Margaret would never fight anywhere again, never fight, nor laugh, nor love….

Nita rose slowly to her feet. Her teeth were set on her lower lip, her eyes large with tears. "It's such a little thing, Dick," she whispered. "Such a little thing… and she saved your life for me, dear."

Nita stumbled away. Wentworth forced his stiff lips to smile, and even the Spider's disguise could not make it sinister. "Did you think I didn't love you, Margaret?" he breathed. "Did you think that... my dear?"

Her eyes were unbearably bright, her smile incredulous.

"You do love me?"

Wentworth bent slowly and pressed his lips to hers. He felt Margaret's slight body shudder in his embrace, her finger tips brush his cheek... Wentworth lifted his head. Margaret was smiling and her eyes gazed into his with a curiously intent look, but they saw nothing. They would never see anything again. Wentworth stumbled blindly to his feet. There was blood on his chest. Margaret's blood.

With a furious curse, Wentworth snatched up guns from the floor. He limped to the doorway and, crouching there, poured hot lead up into the skies, blasting at those circling planes. The stockades were open and scores of women were rushing out into the field, pointing rifles upward. Herman Schull held a girl close in his arms and Nita was circling the fire, hurrying to Wentworth.

"I've called help by radio," she cried. "They'll be here in an hour."

She stood beside Wentworth, her hand on his arm, smiling tenderly at the hurt twist of his mouth.

"Death can be a triumph, too, Dick," she murmured softly.

THE SPIDER

- ❏ #1: The Spider Strikes $13.95
- ❏ #2: The Wheel of Death $13.95
- ❏ #3: Wings of the Black Death $13.95
- ❏ #4: City of Flaming Shadows $13.95
- ❏ #5: Empire of Doom! $13.95
- ❏ #6: Citadel of Hell $13.95
- ❏ #7: The Serpent of Destruction $13.95
- ❏ #8: The Mad Horde $13.95
- ❏ #9: Satan's Death Blast $13.95
- ❏ #10: The Corpse Cargo $13.95
- ❏ #11: Prince of the Red Looters $13.95
- ❏ #12: Reign of the Silver Terror $13.95
- ❏ #13: Builders of the Dark Empire $13.95
- ❏ #14: Death's Crimson Juggernaut $13.95
- ❏ #15: The Red Death Rain $13.95
- ❏ #16: The City Destroyer $13.95
- ❏ #17: The Pain Emperor $13.95
- ❏ #18: The Flame Master $13.95
- ❏ #19: Slaves of the Crime Master $13.95
- ❏ #20: Reign of the Death Fiddler $13.95
- ❏ #21: Hordes of the Red Butcher $13.95
- ❏ #22: Dragon Lord of the Underworld $13.95
- ❏ #23: Master of the Death-Madness $13.95
- ❏ #24: King of the Red Killers $13.95
- ❏ #25: Overlord of the Damned $13.95
- ❏ #26: Death Reign of the Vampire King $13.95
- ❏ #27: Emperor of the Yellow Death $13.95
- ❏ #28: The Mayor of Hell $13.95
- ❏ #29: Slaves of the Murder Syndicate $13.95
- ❏ #30: Green Globes of Death $13.95
- ❏ #31: The Cholera King $13.95
- ❏ **NEW:** #32: Slaves of the Dragon $13.95

THE MYSTERIOUS WU FANG

- ❏ #1: The Case of the Six Coffins $12.95
- ❏ #2: The Case of the Scarlet Feather $12.95
- ❏ #3: The Case of the Yellow Mask $12.95
- ❏ #4: The Case of the Suicide Tomb $12.95
- ❏ #5: The Case of the Green Death $12.95
- ❏ #6: The Case of the Black Lotus $12.95
- ❏ #7: The Case of the Hidden Scourge $12.95

G-8 AND HIS BATTLE ACES

- ❏ #1: The Bat Staffel $13.95

CAPTAIN SATAN

- ❏ #1: The Mask of the Damned $13.95
- ❏ #2: Parole for the Dead $13.95
- ❏ #3: The Dead Man Express $13.95
- ❏ #4: A Ghost Rides the Dawn $13.95
- ❏ #5: The Ambassador From Hell $13.95

THE SECRET 6

- ❏ 1: The Red Shadow $13.95
- ❏ #2: House of Walking Corpses $13.95
- ❏ #3: The Monster Murders $13.95
- ❏ **NEW:** #4: The Golden Alligator $13.95

CAPTAIN ZERO

- ❏ #1: City of Deadly Sleep $13.95
- ❏ #2: The Mark of Zero! $13.95
- ❏ #3: The Golden Murder Syndicate $13.95

OPERATOR 5

- ❏ #1: The Masked Invasion $13.95
- ❏ #2: The Invisible Empire $13.95
- ❏ #3: The Yellow Scourge $13.95
- ❏ #4: The Melting Death $13.95
- ❏ #5: Cavern of the Damned $13.95
- ❏ #6: Master of Broken Men $13.95
- ❏ #7: Invasion of the Dark Legions $13.95
- ❏ #8: The Green Death Mists $13.95
- ❏ #9: Legions of Starvation $13.95
- ❏ #10: The Red Invader $13.95
- ❏ #11: The League of War-Monsters $13.95
- ❏ #12: The Army of the Dead $13.95
- ❏ #13: March of the Flame Marauders $13.95
- ❏ #14: Blood Reign of the Dictator $13.95
- ❏ #15: Invasion of the Yellow Warlords $13.95
- ❏ #16: Legions of the Death Master $13.95
- ❏ **NEW:** #17: Hosts of the Flaming Death $13.95

DUSTY AYRES AND HIS BATTLE BIRDS

- ❏ #1: Black Lightning! $13.95
- ❏ #2: Crimson Doom $13.95
- ❏ #3: The Purple Tornado $13.95
- ❏ #4: The Screaming Eye $13.95
- ❏ #5: The Green Thunderbolt $13.95
- ❏ #6: The Red Destroyer $13.95
- ❏ #7: The White Death $13.95
- ❏ #8: The Black Avenger $13.95
- ❏ #9: The Silver Typhoon $13.95
- ❏ #10: The Troposphere F-S $13.95
- ❏ #11: The Blue Cyclone $13.95
- ❏ #12: The Tesla Raiders $13.95

DR. YEN SIN

- ❏ #1: Mystery of the Dragon's Shadow $12.95
- ❏ #2: Mystery of the Golden Skull $12.95
- ❏ #3: Mystery of the Singing Mummies $12.95

MAVERICKS

- ❏ #1: Five Against the Law $12.95
- ❏ #2: Mesquite Manhunters $12.95
- ❏ #3: Bait for the Lobo Pack $12.95
- ❏ #4: Doc Grimson's Outlaw Posse $12.95
- ❏ #5: Charlie Parr's Gunsmoke Cure $12.95